BUCK

STARGAZER ALIEN MAIL ORDER BRIDES (BOOK 11)

TASHA BLACK

13TH STORY PRESS

13th Story Press PO Box 506 Swarthmore, PA 19081

13thStoryPress@gmail.com

TASHA BLACK STARTER LIBRARY

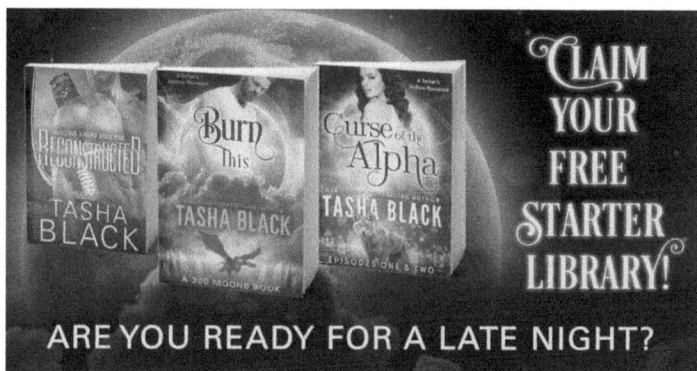

Packed with steamy shifters, mischievous magic, billionaire superheroes, and plenty of HEAT, the Tasha Black Starter Library is the perfect way to dive into Tasha's unique brand of Romance with Bite!

Get your FREE books now at tashablack.com!

BUCK

1

BEATRIX

Beatrix Li took a single step down the dark path and felt ice crunch under her foot.

She knew this was a dream, but it felt so real. Her breath misted in the crystalline air. Stars and planets hung low, casting odd shadows against the rocky terrain.

The world was black and white.

And it was framed - a perfect rectangle with only darkness outside the lines - as if she were standing on a stage.

You're just dreaming about the book again, she told herself.

Beatrix had spent enough time drawing and re-drawing the panels of her graphic novel - she certainly recognized the terrain.

She was inside her own comic panel.

But she shouldn't be able to smell the tang of the copper mines in the air, or hear the shimmering song of the frozen lichen moving gently in the breeze.

She turned back, but behind her was only darkness, outside of the frame.

There was no place to go but forward.

She took another step and another, grateful that there

was a path between the crags. Twin boulders stood side by side in the near distance, like a gateway.

But Beatrix didn't know what lay on the other side.

She had never drawn anything beyond the boulders.

She picked up her pace, unaware if safety lay ahead.

A shooting star blitzed across the sky and she stopped to admire its glittering trail. Beatrix loved drawing light and shadow, which was why she had created this world in the first place, and the humans who visited it.

When she looked down again, she saw a flicker of color near the boulders.

She blinked and it disappeared.

Colored panels were expensive to produce, so Beatrix used them sparingly. This world was meant to be black and white.

But as she got closer to the rocks, she saw another flash of purple.

She began to run. Cold air filled her lungs.

When she got closer, she was startled to see a familiar shape.

A butterfly.

The butterfly fluttered closer. Its violet wings were enormous and webbed with delicate turquoise patterns. It sank, then rose with a dainty flap of those impossibly lacy wings.

She had never seen a butterfly in nature with colors like these. Yet it did not belong on this foreign planet, either. It shouldn't have been able to survive the cold.

The butterfly sailed on a current between the boulders, then hung in the air a moment, as if waiting for Beatrix.

She followed.

The world erupted into a riot of color as soon as she stepped between the massive rocks.

The icy ground turned pale blue. The cliffs and crags took on the sepia-tones of a Pennsylvania winter.

And the air was filled with the trembling wings of a thousand technicolor butterflies.

Beatrix closed her eyes and counted to seven.

When she opened them again the butterflies were still there.

And a man stood before her.

Tall, dark and handsome didn't begin to describe him. He gazed down at her hungrily.

There was something familiar about his brown eyes and the curve of his sensual mouth.

Beatrix tried to place him, but the air was sizzling between them, pulling her closer.

The man reached out to touch her hair.

Shivers of need ran down her spine at his gentle caress.

He cupped her cheek in his warm hand and leaned down toward her, unhurried.

Every cell in her body thrummed in anticipation. She ached for his touch with a desire so fierce it frightened her.

Somewhere in the distance, bells began to ring.

She tried to ignore them and lose herself in the pull of his big body.

But the sound startled the butterflies and they began to dart away.

"Please," Beatrix murmured, but her plea was lost in the sound of the pealing bells.

And the man whose hand still cradled her cheek was fading away, the warmth of his touch dissipating.

Beatrix awoke with tears prickling her eyes.

Her cell phone cheerfully blasted its alarm on the bedside table, oblivious to the fact that it had shattered the best dream she'd had in a long time.

Beatrix slapped it into submission and flopped back down, rubbing her eyes.

She'd never been a morning person.

And today was moving day.

She and her two roommates, and the three aliens they had taken in, had to pack up their belongings from this rented Philly condo and take a car down to Baltimore for the next leg of the Comic Con circuit.

She ran a hand through her hair and tried to decide whether to get up and get moving early like she had planned, or just snooze for ten minutes.

There was a gentle knock at her door.

"Beatrix?" a deep voice said.

Buck...

The dream flashed back before her eyes and she saw what she hadn't before.

She had been dreaming about Buck.

"Give me a minute," she groaned.

She was exhausted, embarrassed and a little turned on. Definitely not a good combination for seeing Buck face to face.

"You said you wanted to be up early," he said through the door.

"I know, I know, I'm getting up," she told him, suddenly feeling decidedly more awake.

"Okay, I'll see you later," he said, sounding a little amused.

Bea waited until his footsteps told her he was leaving. Then she slid out of bed and wrapped a robe around herself.

She had time for a shower. That was one good thing about being up early.

She grabbed her caddy and headed to the bathroom.

Maybe a good soak under the hot water would get her head in the game. Dreaming about a hunky alien wasn't on her agenda right now.

Beatrix's real dream was on the razor's edge of coming true. She had written a break-out graphic novel that was on every teenager's night stand right now. She had a studio interested in making it into the movie version she'd been envisioning ever since she conceived the story.

And she finally had a star, her friend and roommate Kate, who would get butts in the seats, and had the investors interested enough to make the movie happen.

But she'd lost a lot of funding last night.

It was a big price to pay, but her principles were her principles and she would never allow an investor to dictate casting at all - let alone when it came to casting the man who had harassed the star of her film, who also happened to be Bea's friend.

She had two weeks to make up the shortfall.

If Beatrix Li was ever going to be a morning person, now was the time to start.

2

BUCK

Buck had a spring in his step as he walked down the city street.

He had found a way to help Beatrix, if not with the larger problem that was vexing her, at least with her trouble waking up on time.

Though Cecily had cautioned him that Bea was "not a morning person," he had knocked on her door anyway, prompting her to begin her day early enough to accomplish all she wished.

Next he would delight her senses with coffee and doughnuts.

Of course that wasn't the only way in which Buck longed to delight Bea's senses, but he hoped that in time, this way might lead to that other way.

Besides, Buck loved coffee and doughnuts himself, so the task was doubly enjoyable.

Back on his home planet, Buck was a gaseous entity. Like his brothers, he had attained his energy through soaking in the starlight that dappled the rocky planet.

When he was chosen by the leaders of Aerie for migration into human form, he had been fed a nutrient-rich but tasteless formulation in order to maintain his big, hungry body.

It was only on his arrival at the lab in Stargazer, Pennsylvania that he learned of the pleasure and variety of eating.

In addition, he was excited about the fascinating transactional experience of obtaining the foodstuffs, and then the social traditions of eating them.

He arrived at the coffee shop he had visited with Beatrix on several occasions.

"Hey, buddy," said the man behind the counter.

"Hello," Buck said, grinning at the honorific the man had used indicating that they were friends.

Buck could see the glazed doughnuts shimmering seductively behind the glass, but he understood that more talking had to be done before beginning their trade.

"How's it hanging?" the man asked politely.

From all that Buck could understand, this question referred to his penis, which good manners dictated was not supposed to be discussed, particularly around foodstuffs.

"Fine," said Buck carefully. "How is the weather?"

"Ha," the man laughed. "You want some doughnuts, don't you?"

"Yes, please," Buck said. "I'd like twelve doughnuts and three cups of coffee."

"Be damned if I can understand how you have a physique like that when you eat so many doughnuts," the man said, shaking his head as he began to pile doughnuts into a box.

The woman behind the counter stopped pouring coffee to wink at Buck while her employer was bent over the case.

She did not know that Buck's flawless metabolism had been custom-designed for him, as well as the rest of his ostensibly pleasing physique. His looks were the product of good science and good fortune. They had nothing to do with merit.

But he winked back and enjoyed the sight of her cheeks turning pink with pleasure.

He only wished he could earn Beatrix's favor so easily.

"Here you go, son," the man said, handing over the white bakery box.

The woman finished putting lids on the coffees and placed them in a cardboard tray.

Buck tried to focus on his money, instead of thinking about the fact that the man had just called him *son*.

Buck didn't have parents - relationships didn't work that way on Aerie. All of society was like a single brotherhood there.

But he liked the idea of human families with younger and older members having different jobs to protect and provide for the whole.

He handed the man a twenty-dollar bill and got back his change, several more bills and a handful of sparkling coins.

Though he understood intellectually that this money was less than what he'd had before and that the food was appropriately priced, he couldn't help but feel he had gotten the better end of the trade, between the jingling coins and the wonderful breakfast.

"See you next time," the man said, grinning as if he too thought he had the better part of the bargain.

Buck stepped back out into the sunshine and headed home again.

It wasn't home, not really. It was only a borrowed space and they would be leaving it today for another.

But he had already begun to think of home as wherever Beatrix was.

A group of young women wearing backpacks and walking the other direction down the sidewalk stopped talking and observed him wide-eyed.

He smiled at them and they melted into giggles.

He kept walking, satisfied with another sign that all was well with his appearance. It seemed that the only woman who didn't fall apart at the seams looking at him was Beatrix.

She would make a fine mate. Her presence of mind would serve their children well.

But right now, when he was trying to convince her to become his mate, her quiet dignity was a little frustrating.

It wasn't that she was cold to him. Bea was very nice, so nice that at first he thought they would be mated in no time.

Then Cecily had explained to him what flirting was and how good Bea was at it, and he began to worry that all his progress with her might be imagined.

He turned a corner and the breeze blew in just the right way to waft the heavenly scent of the freshly baked doughnuts directly into his face.

Buck sighed with pleasure.

Even if he didn't have complete faith in his own seductive abilities, he had utter confidence in how she would respond to this breakfast.

3

BEATRIX

Beatrix stood in the kitchen eating a doughnut and watching Buck pack up her artwork.

She had stepped out of the shower, still feeling like a wrecked ship, only to have him press a cup of coffee in her hands and point wordlessly to the kitchen counter, where a full box of delicious pastries glistened seductively.

Between the caffeine, the sugar, and the view, she was feeling more cheerful by the minute.

Buck knelt on the floor. He had pushed the coffee table out of the way in order to spread out her drawings. The smaller ones he placed lovingly into a box. The larger ones he rolled and put in tubes.

Beatrix did this all the time, but somehow when Buck did it he made it look like it was choreographed. His muscles bunched and stretched as he worked, biceps rippling, until she couldn't help wondering what it would be like to be the paper he was smoothing so gently with those big hands.

"Penny for your thoughts," Kate teased from behind her.

"Doughnuts," Kirk said happily.

Beatrix was so busy ogling Buck that she had not even noticed them join her in the kitchen.

"Hey guys," she said.

"It's nice to see you awake and alert," Kate said.

Kirk mumbled his agreement around a mouthful of doughnut.

"That coffee's for you, Kate," Beatrix said, indicating one of the two remaining cups on the counter. "Can I assume you were packed up and ready to go hours ago?"

Kate hummed noncommittally as she took a sip of coffee. Bea's friend, and the star of her upcoming movie, was always super organized but clearly didn't want to rub it in.

Which only made her seem even more obnoxiously perfect. Thankfully, Kate had a sense of humor or Bea might not have been able to forgive her. And that would have been a shame, because even though she looked like a blond-haired baby doll, Kate Henderson was one bad ass friend. She had single-handedly salvaged Bea's chance to make her book into a movie. And Bea knew that in doing so, Kate was sacrificing her own retreat from the spotlight and the privacy she had longed for since she was a teenager.

It was a big deal, and Bea was determined to make sure she didn't regret it.

"Where's Cecily?" Beatrix asked.

"Out for coffee," Kate replied. "I swear she has ten best friends to say goodbye to in every city."

Their other roommate, Cecily, was a special effects and make-up pro. Cecily had been in the business a long time and was a total extrovert to boot.

"Is Solo with her?" Bea asked.

Kirk smirked.

Kate elbowed him.

"Yes," she said. "But I wouldn't read anything into it." She leaned her head against Kirk's chest.

For a moment, Beatrix envied their easy familiarity.

Kate and Kirk had gotten together a few days ago, on the last night of the con, and they had been inseparable ever since. Kate had railed against mating with the big alien for a day or two, but from the outside their joining had seemed inevitable.

Beatrix, on the other hand, had never really been in a serious relationship. High school had been a battlefield and the art school she attended afterward had mostly female students and was completely cutthroat. There had been no time to date.

Now she was in her twenties and as inexperienced as she'd been in middle school. She'd learned to flirt like a champion to cover up her lack of experience, but she often wondered where on Earth she was supposed to find a guy who would put up with a woman who didn't even know how a relationship was supposed to work.

"Right here," Buck said from the living room floor.

Beatrix just about spit out her coffee.

"This is where you were sitting when you lost your lucky pencil," he said. "And look."

He held it aloft triumphantly.

It was a simple but perfectly weighted metal mechanical pencil that Bea's mom had bought her for her sixteenth birthday - a bright moment in an otherwise gloomy year.

"Thank you so much," Bea said, dashing over to retrieve it from him. "I couldn't find it anywhere."

He smiled up at her.

For a moment she was transfixed by his deep brown eyes.

Then she remembered herself and snatched the pencil from him, relishing its solid weight in her hand.

"Thank you," she murmured, retreating back to the kitchen in a hurry.

"My pleasure," he said in a way that had shivers going down her spine.

Damned sexy alien.

Maybe *where on Earth* wasn't exactly the right question anymore...

But she had a mission to accomplish. There was no time to moon over him. And it was harder and harder to flirt with him the more she began to realize she might actually like him.

"Well, let me know how I can help you get packed," Kate offered. "We've got a movie to watch on the way that I think you'll like."

"What movie?" Beatrix asked.

"Oh, just wait and see," Kate winked. "Cecily will be back in twenty minutes though, so we'd better boogie."

Bea downed her last sip of coffee and headed to her room to stuff her clothes in the graffiti-covered bag that passed for her luggage.

4

BUCK

Buck felt like a king.

He was tucked into a double seat with Beatrix in a vehicle the women had described as a *stretch SUV*. To their right, Cecily and Solo were in a similar seat, and to their left, Kate and Kirk were snuggled into a double seat of their own.

The gentle motion of the car and Bea's nearness had lulled Buck into a sort of ecstatic stupor.

"I can't believe we're going to Baltimore in this thing," Cecily said with a smile.

"Carol likes me to travel in style," Kate said with a shrug. "Her theory is that if we insist on the best accommodations, we'll also get the best pay."

"Does it work?" Beatrix asked.

"I'm not complaining," Kate said with a smile. "I get paid to stay in a fancy rental and sit in front of a crowd of people getting complimented for work I did when I was fifteen years old. They could literally pay me *anything* and it would feel like I was stealing it."

"Sounds like fun to me," Beatrix said.

"Well, if you think that sounds fun, wait until we get the movie going," Cecily said.

"Seriously, guys, I'm dying to see what the surprise is," Beatrix said.

"What else are you dying to see?" Cecily asked with a smile.

"What are you talking about?" Bea asked.

"We all know who the headliners are at the con in Baltimore," Kate said. "Isn't there one you'd like to spend some extra time with?"

Bea rolled her eyes and slumped back in her seat.

Kate and Cecily laughed.

"I want to talk with Dirk Malcolm about the movie for professional reasons," Bea said. "That's all."

"Oh, okay," Cecily said. "Then hopefully you'll get some *professional* enjoyment out of this."

Cecily pressed the remote and an image filled the TV screen opposite their seats.

It was a galaxy, but not one whose parameters Buck had studied. He didn't see how that was possible. No one on Earth had more celestial knowledge than he did.

Music began to play as names flashed across the screen.

Credits. So it was a movie. Fiction. That explained it.

Buck didn't recognize the first name that popped up, but the second was Dirk Malcolm. This must be one of his movies.

He looked over at Beatrix, trying to figure out what was going on and why she was embarrassed about talking to Dirk Malcolm about her own movie.

She was smiling and shaking her head.

On the screen, the camera panned over a rocky landscape.

"That's Greenfield Gorge," Cecily informed them. "It was practically in my backyard."

"They filmed this in your hometown?" Kate asked. "That's awesome. So you actually got to meet Dirk Malcolm when he looked like that?"

"'Fraid not," Cecily chuckled. "This was shot before I was born. My Aunt Stacy, on the other hand..."

"No way."

"If you believe her stories, she did a lot more than meet him."

"From what I've heard about Dirk Malcolm," Kate said, "I don't doubt it."

There was shared laughter at this, although Buck wasn't exactly sure why.

"So this movie was popular in your youth?" Buck asked, hoping to bring the conversation back to an area he understood.

"It was on TV all the time when I was in elementary school," Bea said. "I must've watched it a hundred times."

"I bet you did," Kate teased.

"I can turn it off if you want," Cecily offered.

"No," Bea said quickly. "You started it up - now we have to see it through."

"Excellent," Kirk said, wrapping his arm around Kate.

Buck leaned back to watch as well, wondering if he dared stretch his arms and then lower one onto the back of Bea's seat, as he had seen done in numerous movies.

Buck and his brothers had watched many movies in preparation for their time on Earth. They were meant to be a cultural reference point and a model for their manners and behavior.

But Dr. Bhimani had told the men that the films they had watched on Aerie were all from an era several decades ago, the 1980s, and that many things had changed on Earth since then.

This movie wasn't quite as old as the ones he'd seen, but it wasn't current either, if it came from a time before the girls were even born. He was curious to see how the movie would differ from those he'd seen.

As he watched the screen, Buck determined that movies had not changed much at all in the time between the eighties and the filming of this one.

He was easily able to follow the plot, which told the story of a young woman, a spaceship mechanic from Earth, who was stranded on a strange planet where the only man who could help her was not human, yet somehow had all the basic human components - two eyes, two arms, two legs, and a muscular abdomen. The main difference seemed to be his skin, which was the pleasing color of a ripe blueberry.

At one point in the movie, the alien bent to repair something on the woman's ship.

"What the heck is he doing? She's the actual mechanic of that ship," Cecily yelled at the screen.

"They have never adequately explained how the ship works," Solo said disdainfully.

"*Nobody cares* how the ship works," Kate said. "We just want to see her fall in love with that big sexy alien."

"I feel like I'm getting déjà vu for some reason," Bea teased, giving Kate and Kirk a significant look.

"I'm not surprised," Kate said, with a straight face. "How many times have you watched this one?"

Bea covered her face with her hands.

Something began to occur to Buck.

He looked at Bea and then at the big blue man on the screen.

Could she be... in love with him?

Was this why her friends wanted to surprise her with the movie?

He didn't want to believe it.

But it felt true.

His stomach felt like it was dropping to the floor of the car.

"Can you believe you're about to meet Dirk Malcolm in real life?" Kate asked Bea.

Bea shook her head slowly.

Cecily laughed.

"Shhh," Kate shushed them, indicating the screen. "He's going to kiss her."

They all watched as the alien on the screen grabbed the mechanic by the shoulders as they shared a lingering kiss.

It was going to be a long ride.

5

BEATRIX

Beatrix took a sip of her wine, leaned back in the garden chair and looked up at the sky through the vines growing on the trellis overhead.

It was hard to believe they were in Baltimore. The rooftop garden on this rental was so lush and isolated, she might have been a million miles away from anyone.

Say what you wanted about Kate's manager, Carol, she certainly came through when it came to five star accommodations.

While the others unpacked, Beatrix and Cecily had come outside to get a little work done.

Not that Bea was getting much accomplished.

She frowned at the notepad perched on her legs.

Instead of the letter she was supposed to be drafting it was covered in doodled butterflies. She couldn't seem to stop drawing them lately, especially when her mind wandered.

"You getting stuck with that?" Cecily asked, looking up from the scaled glove she was working on.

"I'm a writer," Bea said. "Putting together a letter to pitch the movie should be easy."

"It's not the same thing," Cecily said. "But you did write pitch letters to investors before. What's different now?"

Beatrix sighed. She hated to say it.

"It's Carson, isn't it?" Cecily asked.

"Yes," Bea admitted. "He was my first successful pitch and it was in person. One of the people in his group introduced me. Once I had their backing, their participation was one of the main things I led with in these letters. Now that they aren't part of this, it's harder to know how to project confidence that the thing will be fully funded."

"Are you really worried about it?" Cecily asked.

"I need a lot of money, really fast," Beatrix said. "And I went to my most likely prospects first."

"I'll talk to a few people tomorrow," Cecily said. "See if I can find out who's looking for a good project."

Beatrix watched her friend push the needle through the glove she was working on, connecting another iridescent scale to the leather with a stitch so tiny it was invisible. Watching Cecily sew was almost hypnotic.

There was a knock.

"Um, hello?" Bea called.

"Hello," Buck's deep voice floated through the trees. "I didn't want to interrupt your work. But I thought you might want something to eat."

There was a rustling of greenery and then he appeared with a tray in his hands.

The setting sun put a halo around his head.

He smiled down at her and she felt her heart stutter.

Beatrix just stared up at him.

"It's only cheese and crackers," he said, bending to place

the tray on the table between Bea and Cecily. "But we're going to order in as soon as you guys are finished."

"Thank you," she managed.

"Is there anything else I can do to help?" he asked.

Images of him naked, helping her relieve stress in the most pleasant way, streaked through her head.

Beatrix buttoned her lips and shook her head.

"Thanks so much," Cecily said. "This is really nice."

"My pleasure," Buck said. But he was looking at Beatrix.

He winked at her and then disappeared back into the garden in the direction of the apartment.

"He really likes you," Cecily mused.

"Only because he doesn't know any better," Beatrix said.

"Don't joke," Cecily said. "That's one thing you can't do with these guys, Bea. Falling in love is the whole world to them. It's everything."

"I know," Bea said.

She did know. And she was beginning to think that her getting together with Buck might be inevitable. The physical attraction was too much for her to resist.

And he shared her fascination with art, something she had never expected. He'd spent hours watching her sketch. It was odd that he would want to watch her arduous process, and stranger still that she could bear to let him. She generally hid her work from view until it was complete.

Besides the pull of his unbearably hot body, and their shared interest in art, he was also genuinely a nice guy.

And Cecily was right - he really did like her.

If she thought she was going to hang onto her heart in the face of that onslaught, she really was crazy.

She just hoped they could take their time. There was a lot going on in her life with the movie. And Buck had to learn literally everything about being human.

But maybe they could go slowly.

Maybe they could even start tonight...

Cecily began to sew again, her needle dancing between the shimmering scales.

Bea munched on a piece of cheese and watched, mesmerized.

"You know what's funny?" Cecily asked dreamily as if she were hypnotized by her own stitches too.

"Hm?" Bea asked.

"If you got together with him, your funding problem would go away," Cecily said. "As soon as the media got wind that you were with an alien literally *everyone* would want to make your movie."

She looked over at Bea, eyes dancing.

And Bea realized, with a sinking feeling, that her friend was right.

If she were dating an alien, then she could write her ticket.

And just like that, the door that had opened to the idea of getting together with Buck slammed shut again.

Bea was going to be a self-made woman. She had no interest in riding on anyone's coattails.

If her friends could help her get meetings that was one thing. She would still have to land the funding on the merits of her own proposal, based on the strength of her creation.

But utilizing Buck in that way was unacceptable. First of all because she respected him and didn't want to use him. Secondly because she wanted to protect him from the media circus that would surely descend with that kind of publicity.

But the real reason was that she didn't want to use anyone at all.

If she made the film because of alien star power, it would be a spectacle and nothing more. None of the great minds she had dreamed of collaborating with would give her honest feedback to make it a great movie. They would all be kissing up because they wouldn't want to offend the woman with the bona fide alien.

It was going to be hard, but Bea needed to back off from whatever was happening between herself and Buck, at least a little.

At least until she had the film underway.

A little voice in the back of her head screamed that feelings couldn't be put in a schedule.

But, as she often did, Bea ignored the little voice.

She knew what she wanted. And being with Buck wasn't the right way to get it.

6

BUCK

Buck looked around the immense convention hall.

Though he knew this was another city and another comic convention, it was very similar to the Philadelphia Comic Con in appearance, sounds and even smells.

Attendees waited outside in a rainbow of costumes and make-up, talking and laughing excitedly.

He watched from inside the main hall as the vendors prepared for the con to begin. He took in the smell of the popcorn machine and the fluttering of comics and posters being paged through and placed on the tables. And there were the familiar faces of the artists and actors, many of whom were on the convention circuit along with Beatrix and her friends.

"Hey, Beatrix," another artist called. She had pink hair and purple eyeglasses, so Buck had to look at her twice to recognize her. In Philadelphia, she'd had purple hair and pink glasses.

"Hey Q," Bea called back to her.

The woman continued affixing posters to the board

behind her table. Each depicted a small horse with a different logo on its haunches. Bea had explained to Buck that these little horses had been popular a long time ago, but he had already recognized the little ponies from the advertising in some of the films in the time capsule he'd watched to learn about Earth.

He found it comforting to have a frame of reference for some of the things here. There were star fighters from a movie war that he recognized, and familiar superheroes too.

If only this amount of 1980s culture were still relevant in the outside world, he would be much better prepared.

"Are you coming?" Bea asked.

"Sorry," he said, tearing his gaze away from the posters at Q's booth.

They continued back to Bea's table in the corner.

Buck set down the box he was carrying.

"Hang on," Bea said. "That's not right."

She was looking at the number on the table.

"Beatrix," a woman called.

She was an older lady with long gray hair and a pair of dark rimmed glasses.

"Oh, hi, Pamela," Bea said, looking impressed.

"Hello, darling, congrats on your movie deal," Pamela said.

"Well, it's not a done deal yet," Bea said.

"I think I know of a way to get it done," Pamela said with a wink. "I have an opening on the panel at the end of the con."

"Y-you do?" Bea asked.

Buck wondered what this could be about.

"I sure do," Pamela said. "You know the guy who does the CatFace cartoons for Scholastic?"

Bea nodded.

"Well, he's down with the stomach virus," Pamela said, wrinkling her nose. "So he's off the panel. All I need is someone to take his slot. You know Esther Martine is on that panel."

Esther Martine was a huge investor and producer. Her list of blockbusters was as long as her signature black a-line skirts.

"Wow, I'd love to—" Bea began.

"Of course that person would have to take his whole slot, including a featured table at the center of the hall," Pamela said.

"Isn't that—?" Bea began.

"Yes, that's the You-Can-Comic spot," Pamela said.

"But, I don't know anything about teaching kids how to draw," Bea said.

"I think you'll be great at it," Pamela said. "Besides, adventure is good for the soul."

"Oh," Beatrix said.

"Good luck with it," Pamela said, turning on her heel. "I put your number on the table this morning. Let someone else have this miserable corner."

"Thanks," Beatrix called after her.

Pamela merely waved as she marched off to the next aisle.

"Holy crap," Beatrix said, sitting on the table.

"What was that about?" Buck asked.

"The panel at the end of the convention is for the bigwigs," Bea said. "There are a few members on that panel who could even get my movie funded, especially Esther Martine."

"That's wonderful," Buck said.

"But You-Can-Comic is basically drawing lessons for kids," Bea moaned.

"That sounds like fun," Buck told her.

"I've never taught kids before," Bea said. "And I really don't like letting anyone in on my process. It's kind of... personal."

"You let me watch you draw," Buck pointed out.

Beatrix opened her mouth and closed it again.

He waited, fascinated.

"You're the only one," she said. "I've never been comfortable with anyone watching me sketch until you."

His heart throbbed in his chest. She felt as he did, this sense of sanctuary when they were close.

Perhaps he did not need to be as worried about this Dirk Malcolm as he had feared.

"I will help you," he told her.

"How can you help?" she asked.

"I'm not sure," he admitted. "But we will find a way."

She nodded, looking slightly less worried than before.

He longed to touch her cheek, smooth her raven hair behind her shell-like ear.

But the way to help her now was to take action. Their future held plenty of time for tenderness.

7

BEATRIX

Beatrix set her last box of posters on the table as Buck finished affixing her samples onto the wall at the back of the booth.

This table was so much larger than the one she had initially been scheduled for - she was glad she'd brought extra paperbacks and swag.

She looked out over the convention floor. She'd never had such a great location before. It was wild to think about what it would be like if the movie got made, and if people liked it. What would it be like to come to one of these and get mobbed like one of the big stars?

As if she had rung a cosmic doorbell, a man walked past her, a trail of assistants scurrying along behind him. He was tall with reddish-brown hair and piercing blue eyes. And she would have recognized him anywhere.

"Wow," she whispered.

"What is it?" Buck asked.

"That was Dirk Malcolm," she said.

"You wanted to talk to him about your movie," Buck pointed out.

Beatrix shrugged, feeling suddenly overwhelmed.

"You should go talk to him, before everyone comes in," Buck pointed out.

He had a pained expression on his face that was hard for her to interpret. Maybe he was just nervous for her. Though there was no need, she was plenty nervous for herself.

"Beatrix Li," a deep familiar voice said.

She turned straight into the Caribbean blue gaze of Dirk Malcolm.

"My manager said you wanted to meet me," he said, one eyebrow raised.

"Uh, wow," Beatrix said, unable to think of a better response.

"She's friends with your friend Kate's manager, Carol," Dirk went on with a conspiratorial wink. "The ladies who lunch run Hollywood, or so I'm told."

"It's nice to meet you," Beatrix said, finally finding her voice. "I've always admired your work."

Buck made a strange coughing sound behind her, but she ignored him. He was probably trying not to laugh at her. All her friends said she had a crush on Dirk.

"Well I'm a big fan of yours too," Dirk said. "I read *Door to Everywhere* on the plane."

Whoa.

"You liked it?" Bea managed to ask.

"I loved it," Dirk said.

"Wow," she said. "Um, thank you."

"And apparently everyone else loves it too," he said. "I see you're at a different table than the one where they told me to find you. Fame has its perks, am I right?"

"*Doors open in thirty seconds*," Pamela's voice came over the intercom.

"Oh man, I guess I've gotta run," Dirk said. "Maybe catch up with you later?"

"Sure," Beatrix said.

"It was great meeting you." Dirk offered her his hand.

Beatrix reached hers out to shake, but he folded her hand down and kissed her knuckles lightly, just like he had done to the leading lady in the alien movie.

She blinked at him in surprise.

He let go of her hand, winked, and dashed off, presumably to his own booth.

"Wow," Bea said. "That went surprisingly well,"

Buck didn't reply.

She turned to see his eyes were fixed on something across the room.

She scanned the area where he was looking.

The only thing going on over there was a gladiator reenactment group forming. They hadn't been in Philly, but Bea had seen them at the con in Vegas. They seemed like fun guys. All of them were massive and they wore really cool costumes.

"Those are the gladiators. You want to check them out?" she offered. "Go on, I'm fine here."

"Maybe I'll just take a quick walk," Buck said quietly.

"Cool," Bea said.

She watched him leave. It was odd, he seemed almost cold. They had been getting along so well.

Though she had just met one of her heroes, and he had liked her book, Bea found that her good mood was suddenly gone.

She hoped that Buck would be back before the first kids' session. Somehow it seemed impossible to face that without him.

Honestly, she didn't want to spend one minute without him.

Hold onto your panties, her inner critic advised. *Wait until the movie business is done.*

It was good advice.

And it was easier said than done.

8

BUCK

Buck made his way across the floor of the con. Though the doors had just opened a moment ago, there were already hundreds of people pouring in, laughing and trotting toward the tables.

Buck had no real interest in the men Bea thought he was looking at. He had merely been looking away from her, searching for the self-restraint not to beg her not to choose Dirk Malcolm as her mate.

But since she had thought he was interested and she might be watching him, he headed for the men she had called gladiators.

Buck's understanding of gladiators had more to do with the Roman Colosseum than what he was looking at now.

These men were enormous, almost like his brothers, but each had a sort of theme to his costume. One had pink hair and an ax. He wore a leather costume with a rose on it. Another had a black mohawk and a ring through his nose and a shirt with the name of a band on it. A sword with a guitar shaped handle hung from his belt.

All of them appeared to be talking heatedly.

As he got closer, one of them, a man with long blond hair and a pair of brown leather pants noticed him.

"Hey, you're a big dude," the man remarked.

The others looked over at Buck with interest.

"Hello," Buck said politely.

"One of the gladiators made the mistake of eating at the taco truck outside," the man with the leather pants continued. "Do you want to make twenty bucks?"

"I am only one Buck," Buck replied, confused.

The men all laughed.

"One buck, that's... hilarious," the man said. "I'm Adam, but I go by Blaze in the ring. What's your name?"

"Buck," Buck said.

"Oh, I get it now," said Adam. "You're one Buck. Ha. So what do you say - are you in? Will you help us?"

"Well, I'm here with my friend, so I need to help at her table," Buck said.

"Oh, that's fine," Adam said. "We hang out in here during the regular hours of the con to drum up an audience. The actual workouts are off hours."

"What's it about?" Buck asked.

"It's epic," the guitar man said. "We fight in the ring to win the hand of a fair maiden."

"Wow," said Buck, impressed at this idea. "So the winner gets to marry their maiden?"

"Well, that's the gimmick," Adam explained. "You're really just fighting in her honor - no wedding vows required."

"Chicks dig it," guitar guy put in.

Adam nodded and gave Buck a significant look.

"So are you in?" the guy with the rose asked.

"Sure," Buck said. "What do I do?"

"Excellent," Adam said. "Meet us at the stage door at two and we'll begin your training."

They all began shaking his hand, each with a stronger squeeze than the one before.

"I'm Alex," said the guitar guy, crushing Buck's hand when it was his turn.

"Charlie," the rose guy said, giving him a hearty thump on the back.

"Nice to meet you all," Buck said.

"Okay, we gotta go recruit our audience," Adam said at last. "See you later."

Buck's new friends disappeared into the crowd.

He looked back at Bea's table.

Several young women were standing chatting with her and a line had formed behind them.

Bea looked nervous. She was smiling but he could see the tension in her mouth from where he stood.

Buck hurried back to help her.

As he skirted the crowd he couldn't help wondering about what Alex had said.

Chicks dig it.

He wondered if Bea would enjoy seeing him fight in her honor.

Even though she seemed like the type of woman who would gladly fight for her own honor, he felt instinctively that she might like to see him battle for her anyway. What Alex had said resonated within him, as if some instinct of this body of his was telling him an ancient truth about women and entertainment.

He hoped Alex was right.

Buck had told them he would help, and even shaken hands on it.

There was no going back now.

9

BEATRIX

Bea was settling into the routine of greeting fans and moving them through the line.

Buck stood beside her. His posture was relaxed, but she *felt* protected by his presence.

He had shown up again just in time to play interference for her, keeping the most ardent fans from taking too much of her time by stepping in to offer them a pen or a poster.

Beatrix had gone to conventions since she got her first publishing deal. But her main challenge had always been playing it cool when hours passed and no one visited her table.

The steady stream of interested readers this summer was easy to appreciate. And the readers were much like Bea herself, introverts who came out of their shells only to talk about Sci-Fi and Fantasy and graphic novels.

But this mob scene was something new. It had to do with the movie that might or might not get made. And the more outgoing crowd who didn't exactly speak her language was going to take some getting used to. This was a decidedly mainstream group - or as mainstream as you could find at a comic convention.

Bea liked their enthusiasm and curiosity though. And it was cool to think that Sci-Fi might be finding a new and broader generation of fans.

She had just begun to decide this was maybe something she could do regularly when the announcement came.

"*It's time for the day's first set of planned activities,*" Pamela's voice boomed from the intercom.

Bea's stomach dropped to her shoes.

"*Watch a live make-up demonstration with special effects master Cecily Page at Table 58,*" Pamela went on. "*Match your strength against the Intergalactic Gladiators in arm-wrestling at Booth 74. Or hone your budding artist's drawing skills with graphic novelist Beatrix Li at Table 7's You-Can-Comic.*"

"Hey, that's you," the woman Bea was speaking with said with a big smile.

"Yeah," Bea said weakly. "I guess I'd better get to it."

"Neat," the woman said, popping her gum. "Best of luck with your movie. I'm sure I'll see you on the Golden Globes or something."

Bea tried to think of how to respond to that, but the woman was gone already, melted into the departing crowd.

Now there was nothing to do but picture what the heck she was going to do with a bunch of kids who wanted to see how she drew.

"You can do this," Buck said softly from beside her.

She looked up at him and was happily surprised to see from his expression that he felt very secure in what he had just said.

She nodded and took a deep breath and then gathered up the stack of plain white paper she'd gotten from the main lobby as well as a handful of swag pens with her name on them.

Kids were already filling the folding chairs and tables in front of her booth. The area was cordoned off, but the parents and babysitters surrounded the ropes eagerly, as if they were about to watch an MMA fight.

"Should you greet them?" Buck asked.

Shoot. She probably was supposed to greet them.

She nodded grimly to him and headed into the fray.

"Hey kids," she said as nicely as she knew how.

Kids were probably used to women who talked like TV princesses. Well, that wasn't Bea. But she would try.

A little girl at one of the front tables looked up at her, eyes suspicious, mouth furiously gnawing her pen.

"What's your name?" Bea asked.

"Rrrrate-ryn," the girl said around the pen in her mouth.

"Caitlyn?" Bea tried.

"Her name is actually Braitryn," one of the mothers called from over the ropes.

"Oh, I see," Bea replied. "Um, nice to meet you."

She continued past the first few tables, greeting children without trying to learn their names.

Some of the kids were pretty cute. They ranged in age from maybe four or five up to teenagers. Most of them looked like they wanted to be there, but some were rolling their eyes already, which definitely intensified Bea's stomachache.

One pre-teen girl in the back corner at first seemed like an eye roller, but Beatrix caught her glancing up at her when she thought Beatrix was going to turn around.

Bea took in the girl's jeans and Misfits t-shirt and her canvas shoes covered in homemade nail polish drawings and felt a pang. It was a little like seeing a younger version of herself.

She wouldn't have wanted to look a grown-up in the eye in those days either.

When the hell did I become a grown-up?

At last enough seats were filled that Beatrix felt it was time to begin.

"Thanks so much for coming everyone," she said, not loudly enough.

The kids continued to talk with each other.

"Thank you for coming," she said, pumping up her volume. "I'm Beatrix Li. You might know me from my graphic novel, *Door to Everywhere.*"

There were some sounds of recognition.

"Today I'm going to teach you a little bit about drawing a comic panel," she went on. "You're probably thinking that you would never write a two hundred-page graphic novel. But I started just the way you're going to - with a single panel."

The grown-ups murmured their approval from outside the ropes, but the children remained unmoved.

"Everyone, get out your pen and paper," Bea said bravely. "I want you to begin by choosing the setting where you want your panel to take place. Go ahead and decide on a background and see if you can get in one or two land-marks - like a tree, or a spacecraft."

The kids exploded into action. Some began drawing immediately. Others stared at her as if she were speaking an alien language.

Those who had begun drawing almost universally seemed frustrated. Many began crossing out what they had done and some even flipped over the page to try again on the back.

Beatrix froze in place. She had bitten off more than she could chew here.

The room suddenly seemed to close in.

The floor pressed up and the ceiling sank. Braitryn's loud pen chewing sounded closer and closer, as if she were about to chew up Bea herself.

Sweat beaded on Bea's forehead.

"I've got some more paper," Buck's soothing voice said from behind her. "Want to start them with something easier?"

"I-I can't," Bea whispered.

She was frozen in place.

She was going to ruin everything, lose her only chance.

But being in front of people like this... It was too much.

She didn't notice when Buck took center stage. When he cleared his throat loudly she looked up to see him standing there, resplendent in front of the kids, with a ream of printer paper in one arm, a handful of pens lifted high in the other, as if he were some sort of re-imagined Statue of Liberty.

"I'm Buck," he said loudly. "Beatrix's assistant. And she's just let me know that I'm allowed to do an exercise with you today."

She exhaled slowly, looking around at the expectant faces.

"Since I am not as skilled as Ms. Li, I'm going to do something much simpler than what she had in mind," he said. "But I hope you will enjoy it anyway."

He walked over to the front table.

"Here, why don't you hand these out," he said to Braitryn.

The girl promptly dropped her mangled pen and began marching around the space depositing fresh paper on other kids' tables as needed.

"One of my favorite things about *Door to Everywhere* is that the door is in the eye of the beholder," Buck said. "Do you guys know what that means?"

One boy raised his hand.

"Yes?" Buck said.

"It means it depends on who's looking at it," the boy said proudly.

"That is exactly correct," Buck said delightedly. "You are very skilled at idioms for such a small nestling."

The boy blinked at him, then grinned.

"As I was saying," Buck went on. "The magic of the portal is that it takes the viewer to the place he or she most needs to have an adventure. In the case of Shayla, she opens a door covered in lights and buttons, like the switchboard of a spaceship, and she winds up on another planet."

The kids' heads were nodding.

Beatrix was wondering at the idea that Buck had obviously read her book.

And he *got* it.

"But where would you go, if you had a door to everywhere?" Buck was asking the children. "What do you love? What kind of adventure would you have?"

Beatrix recognized what the immediate drumming of fingers and eyes lifting to the ceiling meant.

Those were the sights and sounds of imaginations whirring. She had made those sounds herself - she knew them well.

"Close your eyes," Buck said in the soft voice of a hypnotist. "Close your eyes and picture your very own door. What does it look like?"

Beatrix found herself closing her eyes.

The door was simple with white paneled wood.

"What do you see?" Buck asked. "Can you see the shape

of the door? I've watched Beatrix draw, so I know she begins with shapes, outlines. Let's draw it, let's draw the shape you see in your mind. Don't worry about the details now, just worry about the shape."

Bea's eyes were still closed. She heard the scratch of pens on paper.

"Once you have your shape, think about what comes next," Buck suggested. "Does your door have any decorations? Are there any windows or a doorknocker? If you have a hard time seeing the details, try to imagine what might be on the other side of your door."

But Beatrix already knew what would be on the other side of hers.

That simple paneled door was the one to her room.

And on the other side of it would be Buck.

10

BUCK

Buck walked at Beatrix's side in companionable silence. The setting sun glimmered on the water beside them. They had nearly reached their flat on the Inner Harbor.

Buck's body ached pleasantly from the afternoon of learning to fight gladiator-style with his new friends. Buck was large and strong enough that he hadn't imagined that besting any foe in a feat of strength could be a challenge.

But the Intergalactic Gladiators were a tough bunch, and they possessed skills with weapons Buck had not anticipated.

Adam had said more than once that Buck was a quick study, though. Buck hoped his new friend was correct. He had only a short time in which to improve his skills if he wished to win Beatrix's hand.

He tried not to read anything into her silence tonight. It had been a long day, and she seemed ponderous rather than tense.

Buck was feeling rather ponderous himself after their time together. In some ways, Beatrix was becoming as familiar to him as Aerie's night sky. And in many others, she was a total mystery.

She was a confident woman in private, and yet she was so shy among her fans. She had been unable to talk with the children today.

"Thank you," she said suddenly.

"You are most welcome," he replied politely. "But what for?"

"'I was having such a hard time out there," she said. "I just... I couldn't do it. You were amazing with those kids."

Beatrix's thoughts had not been far from his own.

"No, not really," Buck said modestly, though he felt the kernel of truth in what she said. He had enjoyed talking with the children.

"You really were," she told him. "They felt comfortable with you. And you did such a great job teaching them. I'm really glad you were there."

Buck flushed with pleasure.

They had reached the building. He opened the door and held it for her.

"Thanks," she said, looking up at him.

He wished he could tell her everything he wanted to do for her. Helping with public appearances and opening doors was nothing. He wanted to hold her safe in his arms in her times of sorrow. He wanted to help her accomplish all of her dreams.

He understood the frenzy that drove humanity now, a whole world of desire, distilled down to his own feverish need to fill this one woman with a child of their own.

But he knew his mate enough to know that a display of excessive emotion on his part would only disrupt her own quiet journey toward sharing his feelings.

The whispers of her emotions were there in the soft

expression of her beautiful dark eyes, the pout of her lips, as if they longed to be kissed.

"Let's get upstairs," he whispered roughly, tearing his eyes from hers as they crossed the lobby and stepped into the elevator.

Don't kiss her. Don't scare her off. Let her come to you, he told himself.

But the air between them sizzled with tension.

Beatrix pushed the button to go to the penthouse level.

The machinery whirred and they were lifted up, up in the tiny metal chariot.

Bea bit her lip.

Buck gripped the rail to prevent himself from touching her.

At last the bell dinged to tell them they had reached the top floor.

The others had gone out for dinner, so Buck and Beatrix had the place to themselves for a few hours.

As much as he wanted time alone with her to get to know her better, Buck found himself almost wishing the others were there to distract him from the relentless demands of his heart and body.

Beatrix threw her bag down on the sofa.

"I'm going to take a shower," Buck told her. "I had a good workout with the gladiators. Do you need anything first?"

"I'm fine," she said, shaking her head. "I think I'll send out a couple of funding emails while it's quiet here."

"Good idea," he told her.

He went into the bathroom, closed the door and leaned against it for a moment, willing his body to be calm.

A few minutes later he stood beneath the warm spray of the shower, hoping the water would wash his thoughts away.

He lathered up and couldn't help imagining the hands on his body were Beatrix's instead of his own.

His muscles tensed and his penis was instantly rigid.

Back in Stargazer, he had eased the tension in this organ many times each day in the lab, draining it of its essence as if he were scratching an itch.

But the surges of need he felt now seemed almost unconnected to the pleasant stimulation and relief he'd experienced in the lab.

He slid a hand down to stroke himself, picturing Beatrix in his mind.

The sensation nearly made him moan.

There was a knock on the door.

"Buck?" Bea called to him from the other side.

"Yes," he said, removing his hand from his cock as if he'd been caught trying to steal it.

"Sorry to interrupt," she said. "I was going to order some food. Do you want to look at some menus with me?"

"Yes," he managed to answer. "I'll be out in a minute."

"Cool," she said through the door.

Buck rinsed off in a hurry, cursing himself for his momentary indulgence. Now he was more desperate than ever.

He put on a bathrobe and headed out through the living room to his room to get clothes.

Bea wasn't in the living room. Odd. The menus were spread out on the table, but she was nowhere to be found.

"Bea?" he called.

There was no answer.

Maybe she had gone to her own room to get her phone for ordering.

He went back through the living room to the bedroom hall and knocked gently on her door.

It opened slowly.

Beatrix stood on the other side. She had removed most of her clothing and was wearing only the tiniest scraps of lace over her breasts and her sex.

Buck was unable to rip his eyes from her. He stared in open wonder at the beauty of her small form - tan skin, curving hips and downy thighs.

"Beatrix," he breathed, knowing he should apologize for interrupting her, but unable to find the words.

She grabbed him by the collar of the bathrobe and pulled him into the room.

He instinctively kicked back to push the door shut behind him.

Then she was on her toes, flowing into his arms.

Buck's senses were filled with her, the softness of her skin, the scent of her perfume.

She pressed her sweet lips to his and he swore he heard stars falling from the heavens.

He spread his hands wide and smoothed them down her back, trying to touch as much of her at once as he could.

Bea whimpered and pressed herself against him.

His body roared with need, but Buck willed himself to let Bea take the lead. He had no idea how far she wanted to go, or what was traditional in such a moment. He had no wish to frighten her with his towering desire.

She pulled back slightly and tugged at his collar again.

Buck allowed himself to be dragged over to her bed, let her push him backward.

He lay in the softness of her sheets, looking up at his fierce little mate. The hunger in her eyes was nearly his undoing but he managed to lie still and wait for her, his pulse pounding in his ears.

She crawled on top of him, straddling his hips, and

brushed her lips against his again. He could feel her clever hands tugging at the belt to his robe.

He put a hand in her hair, holding her still so that he could kiss her slowly, thoroughly.

She submitted to his kiss, but she managed to open his robe as he kissed her.

He felt her cool hand against his abs and his whole body screamed for more.

He let go of her hair and she slid downward immediately, trailing gentle kisses down his neck and chest, rubbing her cheek against his belly.

"Bea," he whispered to her.

But she was already wrapping her fingers delicately around his bursting cock. And then he felt the warm, wet heat of her mouth envelope the sensitive tip.

"Bea," he groaned.

Her inquisitive tongue was sliding all over him now, teasing and coaxing him too quickly to the edge.

"You have to stop," he whispered.

She moaned lightly around him and the vibration pushed him even closer.

With the last of his will he slid his hand back into her hair and pulled as gently as he could.

She let go with a disappointed hum, leaving his poor stiff cock pulsing frantically in the air.

"Beatrix, why are you doing this?" he asked, pulling her close.

She lay beside him, covering her face with her hands.

"What's wrong?" he asked.

"I thought... I thought you liked me," she muttered. "I'm sorry I attacked you."

His addled mind took a moment to register what she had said.

Then he began to laugh.

"You don't have to laugh at me," she said angrily.

"I'm not laughing at you," he said, dead serious again at once. "Of course I like you, Beatrix. I don't want to scare you, but my feelings for you are way beyond liking."

"Really?" She sounded less upset but her face was still behind her hands.

"I love you, Bea," he told her helplessly, unable to see her suffer. "I chose you for my mate the night we met."

That was enough to make her move her hands and let him see her face again.

"It doesn't mean you have to love me back or accept me as your mate," he told her. "But it means I have to be very careful about making love with you."

"Why?"

"I have chosen you, and if you accept me we can make love and I will *click* permanently into this human form," he explained. "When that happens, I will be bonded to you forever. But if I *click* with you and you are not ready to accept me... I am not sure what will happen. I might not be able to leave you even if you decided you wanted me to."

"That's intense," Bea said.

"It is," he agreed.

"I like you," she told him. "I like you... a lot. But I'm not ready to get married."

He smiled, his heart filled to bursting.

She liked him. She just wasn't ready yet.

"There's all the time in the world," he told her. "I would never rush you."

"But does this mean we can't even make out unless we're ready to be... mated?" Bea asked.

"You want to make out with me?" he teased.

She reached out her hand to trace his lips with one slender finger.

Buck closed his eyes against the wave of desire that followed in the trail of that tiny touch.

"We can continue," he told her carefully. "But you have to trust me."

"I trust you," she told him.

"Roll onto your back," he told her.

Some ancient instinct in his body gloried at the sight of her rolling onto her back in perfect submission.

11

BEATRIX

Bea rolled onto her back obediently.

Anticipation intensified the desire she already felt, crinkling her nipples against the lace of her bra.

"Good," Buck purred, leaning down to give her another of his maddeningly slow sexy kisses.

He stroked her tongue with his and she felt it all the way down to her sex.

She wondered how much more she could take.

As if he had read her mind, he released her mouth and brushed his lips against her neck, kissing his way down to her aching breasts.

He cupped one in his hand, rolling his thumb against the top where the lace met her skin.

Bea moaned lightly.

He smiled down at her, and peeled back the cup to reveal her breast.

They both looked down at her stiff brown nipple.

"Oh, gods," Buck sighed and lowered his head to kiss her breast.

The sensation was heavenly.

He curled his tongue around her nipple, sucking lightly.

Bea cried out and felt her back arch up.

Without letting up, he released her other breast and caressed it gently with his rough fingers, sending her into a delirium of pleasure.

Too soon, his warm mouth was abandoning her breasts.

She whimpered as she felt his lips caress her belly, and nuzzle her thighs apart.

She opened her eyes and watched as Buck tugged her panties down. She lifted her bottom, and he slid them down her legs and tossed them aside.

Suddenly she felt shy.

Wanton as her behavior had been tonight, it was only the product of her determination to show Buck that she liked him.

Bea had never been great with words alone. It was why she wrote comics instead of novels. For her, communication was about showing, not telling. And she had hoped tonight that her body would tell him what her words could not - that she liked him, she cared about him, she wanted him in her life.

But her real world sexual experience certainly didn't match up with the assertiveness she had shown him.

The reality was that no man had ever put his mouth on her there, and she wasn't sure how it would feel, or whether Buck would like the taste and the scent of her.

She squeezed her eyes shut and waited, hoping that if things went wrong they would go wrong quickly.

But he didn't touch her.

"Are you okay?" he asked.

"Um, yeah," she said, opening her eyes.

"I won't touch you if you don't want me to," he told her solemnly.

She gazed at his unbelievably handsome face. His eyes were hungry.

"No one... no one has ever done that to me before," she admitted.

"I'm glad," he told her, his eyes sparkling. "If you will let me, I will be so happy to be the first man to pleasure you with my mouth. You are the only woman I will ever touch in this way."

"Y-yes, please," she heard herself say.

"Thank you," he breathed, pressing kisses to the inside of her thigh. "Thank you."

Bea let her head fall back on the pillow.

She held her breath as she felt him kiss her center.

"Oh," he moaned against her.

Bea shivered with need.

Buck slid his tongue across her opening.

Desire exploded throughout her body, and seemed to set her on fire.

Buck lapped at her eagerly, stoking the flames.

Bea fought her instinct to lift her hips up to meet his tongue.

But Buck was slowly licking up over her clitoris now, sending pangs of need through her belly and making it harder for her to keep control of her sounds.

She felt him slide a finger against her opening.

He hummed against her clit as he pressed his finger inside.

"Ohhh," she whimpered.

"Does it feel good?" he crooned.

Bea answered by lifting her hips to meet his mouth.

She felt his smile against her thigh, but he gave her what

she wanted, thrusting that inquisitive finger inside her and caressing her pouting clitoris firmly with his tongue in a steady rhythm.

Stars began to form behind Bea's eyes as a wave of lust gathered her up, lifting her higher and higher until Buck finally gave her the spark she needed, suckling gently on her clitoris until the pleasure detonated her like a firework and the ecstasy lit her up from within.

He continued to toy with her, drawing out the last shivers of pleasure, until she pulled weakly at his hair.

He crawled up to her, his mouth glistening with the evidence of what he had just done.

"You are so beautiful," he whispered to her. "Thank you for letting me love you."

"Wow," Bea managed to whisper back.

He smiled, dimples forming over his cheekbones.

"Do you have time for a little nap?" he asked.

"Don't you want me to…?" she asked, embarrassed to say the words.

His jaw tensed, then he exhaled.

"No, I think we'd better not," he said. "Although the idea is… very tempting. But I would like to hold you, just for a little while?"

She nodded and slid over to make room for him.

Buck wrapped his arm around her and she rested her cheek on his chest.

He pressed a kiss on top of her head.

Bea closed her eyes, intending to rest for just a moment.

The last thing she remembered before drifting off to sleep was the sensation of his fingertips lightly caressing her shoulder blades.

12

BEATRIX

Beatrix awoke in a cocoon of comfort, with Buck's warm arms wrapped around her.

There were sounds in the hallway. The others must have come home.

Bea moved to sit up, but Buck held her tightly and deposited a kiss on top of her head.

"Think about what you want to say to them before you dash out of this room," he murmured in her ear.

He had a point.

Her first instinct had been to go dashing out into the hallway to extricate herself from him.

But of course they would know anyway.

And was that really such a bad thing? She and Buck were adults. And she liked him.

"I would never kiss and tell," he whispered into her hair, sending shivers down her spine. "Unless you wanted me to. In which case, I'd go out there singing the news."

"Maybe put some clothes on first," Bea suggested. But she couldn't keep the grin from spreading across her face.

"Excellent choice," Buck replied.

He pulled himself out of bed and pulled on the robe he had come in wearing.

"Oh dear," she said.

"I will gladly wait in here until they all go to bed and then get clothes," he told her. "You can tell them I'm out running an errand."

"It's fine," she said. "I'm not embarrassed."

He smiled as proudly as if she had just handed him an Academy Award.

Beatrix slipped into her clothes and they headed out into the hallway together.

"Hey, guys, how was dinner?" Beatrix called as they entered the living room.

"There you are, sleepyhead—oh..." Kate trailed off as she noticed Buck in his robe.

"Be right back," he said, heading across the living room to the boys' shared room.

Beatrix watched Kate watch Buck until he disappeared into his room.

Kate turned slowly back to Bea.

"So, uh, did you guys have fun while we were at dinner?" she asked.

Beatrix could tell that Kate wanted to ask her if they had formed a mate bond yet.

Bea shook her head slightly.

Kate made a pouting face.

"Give us a little more time," Beatrix whispered with a smile.

"Did who have fun?" Cecily's head popped out of the kitchen.

"I'm gonna let you handle that question," Kate said to Bea, throwing her blonde ponytail over her shoulder.

Cecily's mouth formed a tiny "o" as she looked back and forth between Bea and Kate.

"Did you and Buck—?" Cecily began.

But the guys were pouring out of their room before Beatrix had time to think of how to answer her friend.

Buck was pulling a t-shirt over his head. Bea tried not to drool over his swoon-worthy abs.

"So how did your day go?" Kate asked Beatrix, as if they had not been gossiping about her love life.

Bea shot her friend a grateful look.

"It was exciting," Bea replied.

"Exciting is good," Cecily said, coming out of the kitchen with a bottle of white wine, condensation beaded on the glass, and a pizza box. She placed them on the table.

"We brought you guys back our leftovers," she said over her shoulder as she headed back to the kitchen.

Kirk seated himself next to Kate, wrapping an arm around her.

Kate's relieved smile was radiant, as if she had been in actual pain until he was touching her again.

Bea wondered if their bond could really be so strong, or if she was imagining things.

Buck stood before Beatrix and she patted the seat beside her.

He settled in next to her, and though he didn't put an arm around her, they were tucked in close enough that their thighs were pressed together.

"So how did it go?" Kate asked.

"I kind of got stage fright in front of all those kids," Beatrix admitted.

"But you've done *so* many conventions," Cecily said, coming back in with three glasses.

Solo followed her with three more. He set them on the table and sat next to Cecily.

"This was different," Bea said. "You know I don't do well with showing my process. Besides, kids are different. They have built-in bullshit detectors."

"So what did you do?" Kate asked.

"I didn't," Beatrix said. "I froze up. Thank goodness Buck was there. He's fabulous with kids."

"It was nothing," Buck said.

"It was not nothing," Bea told him firmly.

"You're going to have to get used to the spotlight, Bea," Kate said.

"What do you mean?" Beatrix asked.

"I mean this movie," Kate said. "You can't make a big movie and not wind up with a lot of people paying attention. You have to learn to put your shyness aside."

"I'm not going to be *that* famous," Bea said dismissively.

"Maybe, maybe not," Kate said. "But no matter what happens with the movie, when the truth comes out, Buck is going to be *crazy* famous. Way more than I've ever been. How are you going to deal with that?"

Beatrix felt her throat tighten.

"I'm not going to be famous," Buck said firmly.

"You can't hide forever," Kate said.

"I can and I will," Buck told her. "Keeping my origins secret is the most important thing to me. Not just to protect my brothers back in Stargazer and the others who escaped, but also for myself. I would never, ever want to be the object of public curiosity."

Bea looked up at him and saw in his eyes that he was serious.

And crazy as it sounded, she was sure that if he wanted to live as a regular human it was likely possible. He was huge and unusually good looking, but he had an easygoing nature and a sweetness that made him seem less *alien* than his brothers.

She smiled up at him and leaned her head against his shoulder for a moment.

"To privacy," Cecily said handing out the glasses she had poured.

"To privacy," they all repeated, clinking glasses all around.

"Not to change the subject, but I did a little digging today," Cecily said.

Bea felt her heart skip a beat. Cecily had been trying to get investor leads for her.

"I had two people who seemed pretty interested, but neither of them got back to me," Cecily said. "It's weird. I mean I know we're at a con, but usually these guys would be all over a chance to get in on the ground floor of something this promising."

"It's my fault," Kate said suddenly. "You thought that bringing me on as the star would push your project over the edge. But, of course no one wants to work with me if Spencer is out there saying I'm hard to work with. He's an idiot, but his dad is a big deal in this business. If it helps you, I can step down."

"That's not it," Bea said firmly. "And even if it were I wouldn't care. I can't wait to have you in this movie. It's a dream come true. We will find the money."

Kirk kissed the top of Kate's head and Bea was relieved to see her perk up a little.

So Bea might have to work a little harder to get the funding. That was fine. She had a brilliant star, good friends, and a great guy by her side. Everything would fall into place.

13

BUCK

Buck leaned against a table the next day, watching Bea work.

She was walking among the tables of children, greeting them with a quiet confidence that made his heart swell with pride.

It was hard not to wonder what Bea would be like with children of her own.

Something Buck hadn't shared with her yet was that it would not be enough for them to be mated. He was supposed to experience human life in full, not only as a mate but as a father.

Yesterday, the thought made him anxious. He wasn't sure how Bea felt about kids after she had frozen up in front of them. But today he could picture her coming around on the subject.

Some of the kids at the tables now had returned after the morning session she'd taught. They liked her a lot.

Buck could hardly blame them. He liked her a lot too.

"Close your eyes," she was telling them. "I want you to picture a tree. It can be a young sapling or an ancient tree, big or small, but it is your tree. In *Door to Everywhere* Shayla's tree was a willow, like the one she remembered from the pond on her grandmother's farm."

He looked out over the young faces, the closed eyes and peaceful expressions.

"Okay, you can open your eyes now," Bea told them. "Think about the shape of your tree. Don't worry about the details."

Pens began scratching the paper.

She looked over at him and her smile made him feel almost dizzy with love.

He had slept in his own bed in the room with Solo last night. Though he longed to join her, he didn't trust himself not to fall prey to his body's temptation.

But soon, soon he hoped she would be ready to accept him.

She walked through an aisle of tables chatting with the kids, tapping a slender finger on something she liked.

The child whose page had been touched smiled up at her in delight.

"I guess this is going okay," she said, joining Buck at the table.

"It's going way better than okay," he told her. "Great job."

"It's easier with you here," she said. "But I understand if you want to go and stretch your legs."

"I wouldn't want to be anywhere else in the world," he said, shaking his head.

She looked down at her shoes and he wondered at how she could still feel embarrassed and shy around him when she knew he loved her.

One of the kids raised his hand and she was off again, her dark hair swinging behind her.

Soon it would be time for her lunch break. Buck was

hoping that she would agree to eat at one of the restaurants downstairs.

He had learned that Beatrix's surname was of Chinese origin, and the restaurant he had in mind had a sign declaring that it served authentic Chinese cuisine. Buck was eager to learn more of Beatrix's heritage, and also to taste the food that had such an enchanting smell.

The work was pleasant but his belly was rumbling. Besides, he was looking forward to spending some time alone with his intended, hearing her thoughts about all that had passed during their day.

"Great job, guys," Beatrix called to the children. "Our time is up for now, but feel free to come back later this afternoon for the final session."

"Somebody's feeling more confident today," a man's voice said.

Buck turned to find Dirk Malcolm standing beside him.

"Yes, she's having a great day," Buck agreed. He was glad to find that his happiness expanded enough to envelope this man, whom he had once seen as a rival.

Bea walked over to join them.

"Hey, Mr. Malcolm," she said.

"Call me Dirk," he said, smiling at her in a familiar way that Buck didn't like.

"Cool," Bea said. "How were your signings?"

"I hate to brag, but I was mobbed," Dirk said. "And I can see your day went well."

"Yeah," Bea said, looking at Buck. "It was pretty awesome."

"Listen," Dirk said leaning in. "I'd like to have lunch with you."

"We'd be glad to have lunch with you," Bea said right away.

Dirk winced.

"Sorry, man," he said to Buck. "But I want a little privacy with the lady to talk shop. Hope you understand."

A river of molten lava flowed through Buck's chest. He gasped.

Jealousy.

Surely it couldn't be. No mere emotion could cause this kind of pain.

But there was no explanation. His heart was beating, and there was no lava in the convention hall.

Beatrix opened her mouth.

"That's fine," Buck said, before she could speak. "I wanted to check in with my brothers."

"Neat," Dirk Malcolm said with a dismissive expression. "Shall we?" he asked Bea.

"Sure, okay," she said. "You want me to bring you back anything?" she asked Buck.

But he was too angry to do anything but shake his head.

She wants to talk business with him. Maybe he can help her get the money to make the movie, his more reasonable mind argued.

But the wordless emotion in him raged and roared in response.

14

BEATRIX

Bea sat across from Dirk Malcolm at the cafe.

As unbelievable as she would have found this scenario just a few years ago, even more unbelievable was the fact that he seemed to be expressing a real interest in her project.

"At any rate, I'm very glad to know that you're being careful about the film," Dirk said. "So many authors would just sign those rights away without maintaining any artistic control."

"Here's your lunch," a waiter said, sweeping in with two sandwiches.

"Thank you," Beatrix said.

The waiter ignored her, instead gazing adoringly at her companion.

"I hope you don't mind me saying, I'm such a fan of your work, Mr. Malcolm," he said in a slightly strangled voice.

"Thanks, kid," Dirk said magnanimously. "I get that a lot."

The waiter grinned and then dashed off.

"Fame," Dirk said, shaking his head. "Am I right?"

Bea had no earthly idea, but she was glad she wasn't the only one freaking out over Dirk Malcolm.

"Anyway, Beatrix, I'm sure you're wondering why I invited you," he said.

She nodded slowly, praying he wouldn't hit on her. Not that he wasn't still hot, but she considered herself spoken for. And if he hit on her, it would undermine every good thing he'd just said about her book and her business savvy.

"This isn't easy to say, so I'm just going to spit it out," he said. "The reason you're having a hard time getting funding is that Carson is blackballing you."

It felt like someone had punched her in the gut.

"I know I would want someone to tell me, if I were in your position," Dirk went on. "The problem is not the book or the script, or you. The issue is that one of the biggest names in the industry is saying that anyone who invests in your project will be barred from investing in any of his for the foreseeable future."

Beatrix took a deep breath and then let it out again slowly.

"Are you okay?" Dirk asked kindly.

"Yeah," she said, nodding. "It's not what I wanted to hear, but at least I know why I can't get any traction."

"You just need to regroup," Dirk suggested.

"What do you mean?" Bea asked.

"Look," Dirk said, leaning in. "I know Katie Henderson is your friend and she'd be fantastic in that role, but she's not the only actress in Hollywood. And frankly, she hasn't acted in almost ten years—"

"I'm going to stop you right there," Bea said. "Using another actress is a non-starter for me. I'm not going to let Carson win by bullying."

Dirk shrugged. "Okay, then you'll need to strategize. The usual round-up of funding won't work in this case."

"So what do I do?" Bea asked. "What would you do?"

"Well, there's private money," Dirk said. "Do you know anyone who's independently wealthy and interested in the arts?"

Bea shook her head.

"I didn't think so, but it's always worth asking," Dirk said. "The only way to get traditional Hollywood money invested on this project with Carson against it is to guarantee success."

"Okay," Bea said. "I don't have a crystal ball, but I will do what it takes to make the best movie I can. And the books have a good following, so that's a built-in audience."

"Here's another hard truth for you," Dirk said. "I'm sure the readers of your graphic novels are awesome, but there aren't enough of them to make this movie a big money-maker. To attract investors in spite of Carson your film would have to *promise* a big return."

"How can I possibly promise something like that?" Bea asked.

"You need to tie this film in with something bigger, something *way* bigger," he said.

"Like what?"

"Set your sights *on the stars,*" Dirk said significantly, then leaned back in his chair to watch her reaction.

Beatrix's mouth fell open slightly as she tried to figure out how he'd put it together that Buck was an alien.

They had been so careful.

"I mean me, of course," Dirk added, winking at her.

Oh.

Oh.

"Y-you would be willing to be in this movie?" Bea stammered. "Despite what Carson is doing?"

"I'd be delighted," Dirk said. "Like I said, I love the book."

"Thank you so much," Beatrix said. "I can't tell you how much this means to me.

"It's my pleasure, Beatrix," he said. "If I don't use my star power for good, what's the point of having it?"

"It's amazing to meet someone whose work I've admired on screen for such a long time," Bea said. "And it's truly amazing to realize that you are an even bigger hero off the screen than you are on it."

"God, I wish you would write that down so I could put it on my blog," Dirk said. "Now let's eat before that kid comes back and asks us how the food is."

As they dug into their meal, Bea was starting to feel like she could see the light at the end of the tunnel.

15

BUCK

Buck sat beside the other gladiators in the gymnasium in the wing next to the main hall of the convention center. He drank water out of a plastic mug that said *Intergalactic Gladiators ROCK* and tried to soothe his jangled nerves.

In spite of a powerful lunchtime workout, he was still filled with restless energy at the thought of Beatrix being out for a private meal with Dirk Malcolm.

"Let's hit it again," Adam said.

They all got up and grabbed their weapons.

"Simple swordplay - thrust and block, you guys know what to do," Adam shouted.

This exercise was among Buck's favorites. It was a precision drill, not a stamina exercise, so the gladiators often gossiped during it since they weren't winded.

"So, how's Tiffany?" Angel asked Adam, waggling her eyebrows as she thrust her staff at him.

Angel was one of the largest gladiators. She was even taller than Buck and her muscles rippled as she worked, sending her long pink hair back over the cherub wing tattoos on her shoulders.

"Meh," Adam replied, blocking her with a grunt.

"What happened?" Angel asked.

"I don't really know, but I saw her hanging out with Jason Washington," Adam said.

"The guy from that TV show?" Angel asked.

Adam nodded.

"Damn," Alex said as he thrust his guitar sword at Buck. "It's nice to be beefcake, but it's the scrawny big-time actors who get all the girls."

Buck blocked Alex's sword and thrust his own.

"Is Dirk Malcolm a big-time actor?" he asked as casually as he knew how.

"Oh, he's the *worst*," Angel said immediately.

"He is like the worst one," Adam agreed. "Lock up your girlfriend when he comes around, for sure."

"Not to change the subject, but you guys are coming to my party, right?" Alex asked, thrusting at Buck.

Buck nearly missed the block, still thinking about Dirk Malcolm being the worst.

"You okay, dude?" Alex asked.

"Yeah, fine," Buck replied. "What party?"

"Oh-ho, just you wait, it's going to be epic," Alex said. "And you're totally coming."

The last thing Buck wanted to think about was a party.

"I don't even have a car or anything," he said.

"I'll give you a ride," Angel offered. "You don't want to miss this. There's *always* a party the night before the tournament. And Alex makes parfait jello shots."

The others made noises of excitement.

But Buck had a sudden thought.

The movies had taught him something about women.

He had already shared his wisdom with his brother, Kirk, with excellent results. The wisdom boiled down to this:

There were three ways to make a woman realize how much she liked you.

The first was with flowers.

The second was giving her space - that was what Kirk had done to win over Kate.

The third thing was to make her jealous by letting her see you with another woman.

Buck stole an appraising gaze at Angel.

She was truly a magnificent woman - strong, enthusiastic, with glossy pink hair and intricate tattoos. She was even large enough that Buck felt being seen with her might be almost as good as being seen with several smaller women.

So long as there was no misunderstanding on Angel's part about his intentions, Buck felt that Angel was the perfect woman to make Beatrix experience a wave of jealousy that would bring her to her senses.

"I'd love a ride as long as it doesn't cause you trouble," he told Angel. "My girlfriend is busy tonight so she can't come."

He hoped that mentioning a girlfriend would make his intentions clear.

"No problem," Angel said, thrusting mightily at Adam. "Just write down your address for me before you go. And if your girlfriend's plans change we'll bring her along. She'll love Alex's party - everyone does."

"Thank you," Buck said.

"Don't mention it," Angel replied, blocking Adam so hard that he nearly fell over.

"Nice one," Adam said.

Angel really was an incredible woman.

He hoped Beatrix wouldn't be *too* jealous.

16

BUCK

Buck stood between his two brothers in the bedroom he and Solo shared. Kirk was now spending his nights in Kate's room, which made Buck both happy and envious.

The view over Baltimore's Inner Harbor was stunning, but he could hardly enjoy it when his brothers were unhappy with him.

"Why would you do this?" Kirk asked.

"It's only a ride to a party," Buck said. "I'm not getting married."

"But it seems unsporting to attend a party with another woman when you and Bea have been growing closer," Solo said with a frown.

"She went to lunch with Dirk Malcolm *alone,*" Buck pointed out for the third time.

"You keep saying that," Kirk said. "But how do you know it was romantic?"

"He wanted to have lunch with her privately," Buck said. "Why would he need to be alone with her if it's not romantic?"

"That is not good," Kirk agreed.

"What about her movie?" Solo asked.

"If he wanted to talk about the movie, would he have cared if I was there?" Buck asked. "He said he wanted to talk shop alone with her, but his eyes said he wanted something different."

"Beatrix is a woman of character," Solo declared. "No matter what he wanted, you can be sure she did not give it to him."

Buck felt the truth of this. But he also remembered the look on her face that night they had all watched that Dirk Malcolm movie in the car.

He paced alongside the big window of their room, clenching his fists.

"He's thinking of Bea's crush," Kirk told Solo quietly.

"What are you talking about?" Solo asked.

"What if it's not just a crush?" Buck asked.

"When we were in the car, watching the movie, do you remember how the women were teasing Bea about the alien in the movie?" Kirk asked Solo.

"Is that what they meant?" Solo sounded surprised.

Buck felt momentarily sorry for his brother, Solo, who understood so few of the humans' subtleties. He hoped that more time among them would ease his transition.

"Buck, a teenaged crush and the love of a mate are two very different things," Kirk pointed out. "If you are concerned that Bea has feelings for this man, the best thing to do is to talk to her about it."

"I'm afraid of what she will say," Buck admitted. "But if I let her feelings tell her what she wants then she will know she is meant to be mine."

"Is this your three-things-about-women business again?" Solo asked. "Why don't you just buy her some flowers?"

"Or give her a little space?" Kirk suggested.

"No," Buck said. "I have felt this jealousy emotion and I know it will bring her to her senses. Besides, I promised the gladiators that I would attend their party."

"I hope it works," Solo said thoughtfully.

"Why? Are you thinking of trying it on Cecily?" Kirk asked, looking unhappy.

"No," Solo said with a dreamy expression. "Cecily will require no tricks. She already loves me. She just hasn't noticed yet."

In spite of his predicament, Buck found himself laughing.

He was happy when Kirk and even Solo joined in.

They were doing their best. Surely Bea and Cecily would realize that he and Solo would be loyal and protective - the perfect mates.

Bea just needed a little nudge.

"So what is a person supposed to wear to a party?" he asked his brothers.

"Your finest clothes," Solo said immediately.

"What kind of party?" Kirk asked.

Buck considered. "There will be parfait jello shots," he offered.

"What are those?" Kirk asked.

"I have no idea," Buck admitted.

"They sound fancy," Kirk worried.

"We don't have fancy clothes," Buck said.

"Well, Dr. Bhimani did give us that money for an emergency," Solo said. "Maybe we can use some of it for your clothing."

"Good thinking," Kirk agreed.

The other two watched as he slipped an envelope with

Dr. Bhimani's looping handwriting on it out of his duffel and slid it into his pocket.

"Let's do this," he said, pleased by his effortless use of the Earth expression.

They slipped out of the room and through the common living room.

"Where are you guys going?" Kate asked from her place on the sofa next to Cecily.

"Oh, just a little shopping," Kirk told her. "Can we bring anything back for you?"

"I'm fine," Kate replied.

"I'm fine, too," Cecily said. "Bea's in the shower, I'll let her know where you went when she gets out."

Buck felt a momentary pang, but held fast.

He was doing what he had to do to get into her heart forever.

17

BEATRIX

Bea sat on the sofa, drawing butterflies again.

She'd been drawing them absentmindedly ever since having that crazy dream. This batch was in colored pencil, and she was getting good enough they looked like they could practically float off the page.

Cecily sat beside her, stitching more scales onto the costume she'd been working on.

Katie was curled up with her laptop reading the gossip columns out loud to them. So far there was no mention of Carson.

What they were all *really* doing was trying to pass the time with the boys out of the house.

As far as Bea could remember, they had never gone anywhere without one of the women since their arrival. She hadn't even known they had money to shop with.

"*Rumor has it a certain comic book author and her child star ingénue are running into money troubles with their pet project,*" Kate read. "*They say funding is in the works. But word on the street is that a big guy with a big grudge has pulled his support. Better pinch your pennies, girls, money's gonna be tight.*"

"Well, there's your answer," Cecily said.

"It doesn't say he's actively blackballing me," Bea pointed out.

"It can't say that," Kate said. "Even in this vague form they can't risk being sued for libel."

Bea's heart sank. Kate was right, of course. And Dirk had no reason to lie to her anyway.

The sound of the guys at the door made her smile in spite of herself.

It was funny how just knowing Buck was near made it easier to deal with the roadblocks to her career.

The guys came in, Kirk followed by Solo.

Then Buck.

He wore his usual jeans but with a white Oxford shirt and tie and a navy-blue blazer. His too-long hair was slicked back with gel.

"Wow," Bea said. "You look great."

Buck grinned, then he straightened his face into a more serious expression. "I am going to a party," he said.

"Oh," Bea said. "What party?"

"The Intergalactic Gladiators invited me," he said. "There will be parfait jello shots. I'm going with Angel. She's going to pick me up in a few minutes."

Bea felt a pang of hurt. Why would he go to a party without her? She hadn't even had the chance to tell him about her lunch with Dirk.

And she didn't like the sound of this woman, Angel. When had Buck had a chance to meet another woman? And hadn't he told Bea that he loved her?

Maybe love meant something different to an alien.

To Bea it meant forever.

She stared at him, unable to respond.

Cecily put a hand on her knee.

"Hey, Bea didn't get to tell you what happened at lunch today," Kate said brightly.

"That's true," Buck said. "But Dirk Malcolm wanted to speak to her privately, so she may not want to share what was said."

"Oh, no, it's fine," Bea said. "It's great news, actually. He agreed to be in the movie."

She only wished her voice didn't sound so small and sad.

To her surprise, Buck didn't even congratulate her. He merely nodded, his mouth a narrow line.

The doorbell rang before anything more could be said.

Solo turned and opened it.

An enormous woman stood on the other side.

"Hey," she called out. "Is Buck here?"

"Yes, I'm here, Angel, please come in," Buck said.

Bea swore the woman had to duck to get in the door.

"Hi guys," Angel said, looking around with a big smile. "Nice place."

"Thanks," Kate told her. "We hear you guys are going to a party."

"Yeah, Buck's going to have the night of his life, right, big guy?" Angel asked Buck, tossing her silky pink mane over her shoulder.

He grinned back at her.

Beatrix balled her hands into fists and managed not to scream.

"Anyone else want to join us?" Angel asked, looking around.

"No, we're fine," Bea managed.

"Well, we've gotta fly then," Angel said. "Nice seeing you all."

When Angel turned around, Bea could see the wings

tattooed on her shoulder blades peeking out of the tiny tank top she wore.

"Good-bye," Buck said.

Bea couldn't even look at him.

The door shut behind him and the five remaining friends sat in utter silence for a moment.

"I think we need a girls' night," Cecily said suddenly.

"Which type?" Solo asked.

Everyone looked at him.

"The type where you go out and drink wine and yell?" he asked. "Or the type where you put your hair in curlers and talk about boys?"

"The eighties were kind of a rough time for women in movies," Cecily observed. "But if we have to choose, I think we'll have the drinking kind."

"Tell you what," Kirk said. "Why don't you order in? There's wine in the kitchen. I think I'm going to catch up to those guys and take Angel up on her offer to bring us along. I want to keep an eye on Buck. What do you say, Solo?"

"This is a wise plan," Solo declared. "Enjoy your girls' night."

The two took off in hot pursuit of Buck.

"You heard him, there's wine in the kitchen," Kate said, hopping up and heading for the refreshments.

"I'll order a pizza on my phone," Cecily said. "Does that sound okay?"

"Sure," Bea said, thankful that her friends were there to keep her company on this long and confusing night.

Kate returned from the kitchen with three wine glasses and a bottle just as Cecily put her phone down.

"Are you going to be okay?" Kate asked Bea gently.

"I'll be fine," Bea said. "It's just freaking typical."

Kate looked to Cecily and back to Bea again.

"Um, *nothing* about what just happened was typical," she replied.

Cecily giggled and Kate giggled too.

"Well, it might not have been *typical,*" Bea allowed. "But it was awful."

"Have you ever seen such an enormous woman?" Cecily said wonderingly. "I wonder how many scales I'd need if I wanted to make a costume for her."

"You know, not everyone is hung up on traditional body types," Bea said. "I happen to think she was gorgeous."

"Yes, she is, and she's *twice* the woman you are," Kate said, bursting into giggles.

Cecily laughed too.

"I'm with you on the body type thing, Bea," Cecily giggled. "But you have to admit that's a good joke. You know? Because you're so tiny, and she's so tall."

Cecily melted into helpless laughter.

"Besides, I don't even think she's into him like that," Kate said. "Seriously, did you see the way she was eyeing up Cecily?"

"Oh, no," Cecily said immediately. "That's just my shoulders. She was probably only checking me out for gladiator purposes. I spent all of college fending off a roller derby team. Apparently, I have wide fighting shoulders."

Beatrix began to laugh in spite of herself.

"Oh, *that* made you laugh, huh, Miss Body Issues?" Cecily pretended to be offended but she was grinning.

"Thank you," Bea said. "Really, I don't know what I would do without you guys."

"Hey what are friends for?" Kate asked, handing out wine glasses.

"Here's the thing, all jealousy aside," Bea said slowly. "I think maybe this is for the best."

"What do you mean?" Cecily asked.

"My career is taking off, I hope," Bea said. "Or at least it has a chance, which is more than I've ever been able to say before. Meanwhile, Buck wants privacy. I'm not saying I don't care about him, but... the timing is all wrong. And with these guys it's now or never, right?"

"Oh, Bea," Kate said, wrapping an arm around her shoulder.

"Maybe he's better off with Angel," Bea said, though tears blurred her vision. "He likes the gladiators. And her life seems so much simpler than mine."

"At least he'd be in no danger from prowlers," Cecily quipped. "Did you see those muscles?"

"Cecily," Kate hissed.

"Sorry, Bea, that was low-hanging fruit," Cecily said. "But truly, I hope you'll sleep on this. Things may look different in the morning."

Bea nodded, wiping tears from her eyes with the heels of her hands.

She didn't want to disappoint her roommates.

But her mind was made up.

18

BUCK

Buck stood behind the audience at the Intergalactic Gladiator tournament's opening round.

The audience sat on bleachers in the gym where the gladiators had been working out for the last two days. The crowd looked pretty excited, at least as much as Buck could tell from behind.

He wished he could locate Beatrix among the faces, but the lights were already dimming, soon it would be his turn to go up and joust.

She'd been asleep on the sofa when he came in from the party.

He felt bad that she had waited up for him, but he hoped it meant that she had felt jealous, and was ready to be honest about her feelings for him.

Rather than waking her, he'd left a note inviting her to come to the tournament.

If luck was with him, he would win, and between the jealousy last night and then seeing him victorious in her honor today, the interest she had felt would be rekindled.

If not, he didn't know what he would do.

As he watched her sleep last night, her soft cheek pressed to her hand against the sofa cushion, his heart had been full. The pull he felt had nothing to do with the glow of her skin or the luster of her dark hair in the lamp light.

It was Beatrix he loved. She was small and fierce and strangely shy at times. Her personality refracted like starlight playing on the south bay of Aerie. He was fascinated by her changeability.

But there was a core of loyalty in her. She had waited up for him. In spite of the jealousy, in spite of the fact that he knew her feelings might have been hurt, just as his had been when she left with Dirk Malcolm.

Some part of her knew what he had been trying to tell her. They were meant for each other. She was his mate. It was no longer a choice.

"Thank you for coming out everyone," Adam was saying into the microphone as the lights on the audience went completely out. "I would make a big speech or something, but we all know what you came here for!"

"*Joust-ing, joust-ing*," the audience roared.

"You asked for it," Adam said. "First up is Alexander the Great Guitarist. His axe shredded in Vegas and he's here to rock and roll in Baltimore."

From the other side of the gym Alex waved to Buck and then jogged up to the stage. He was wearing rock star clothing with his hair teased up. His guitar-shaped weapon shimmered in the stage lights.

"Facing off with Alexander the Great is our newest gladiator," Adam continued. "He's new to the joust but he's not new to the world of finance. Meet The-Buck-Stops-Here!"

Buck jogged up with his sword as best he could in the suit they had given him to wear. The enormous golden plastic dollar sign necklace around his neck kept bouncing up to hit him in the chin. He felt very fortunate that it wasn't real gold.

On the stage there were two pillars, each about two feet off the ground. On each pillar was a small round platform.

Alex had already climbed onto his platform. He stood there, gazing down ominously at Buck with a terrible sneer.

This was odd, because Buck had just been at his party last night, where Alex had wrapped an arm around Buck and declared that they were brothers. *This guy,* Alex had exclaimed, shaking his head. Buck had assumed that was a good thing.

Buck climbed onto his own platform.

"Oh, ladies and gentlemen, you can see the animosity between these two fierce warriors already," Adam crooned into the microphone. "This promises to be a serious fight, and serious entertainment."

It suddenly occurred to Buck that Alex might be pretending to be angry in order to stir up the crowd's emotions.

He fixed Alex with a mighty glare.

Alex lunged toward him slightly. But he also winked at Buck with his upstage eye, which was out of sight of the audience, as if to say it was all in good fun.

"Bow to each other," Adam said.

Buck and Alex bowed.

"And to the audience," Adam said.

Now was his chance.

Buck scanned the audience for Beatrix.

He almost missed her because she wasn't sitting in a seat at all. She stood in the aisle near the back bleachers, watching him with a blank expression on her beautiful face.

Alex cleared his throat.

Buck bowed quickly to the audience, then turned back to his rival.

"Okay, gentlemen, time to *goooooooooooo*," Adam roared.

Alex instantly thrust at Buck with his sword.

Buck was so surprised he didn't think to block. He managed to lean out of the way at the last second.

The crowd cheered.

He thrust his sword immediately at Alex, who blocked so hard Buck nearly fell.

He managed to stick to his platform, but it was Alex who attacked next with a mighty jab.

Buck gathered all his strength and blocked as hard as he could, hoping he could loosen the weapon in his rival's hand.

He realized the moment he had gone too far, but it was too late.

While Buck was extended outward for his block, Alex stepped forward sideways and tucked his blade under Buck's, pulling him slightly forward.

The platform beneath him began to tilt as his weight came forward to compensate for the pull.

And he slid off onto the stage.

His part in the tournament was over before it had really begun.

The crowd cheered for Alexander the Great as Buck looked for Beatrix.

But all he caught of her was her retreating silhouette exiting through the back door of the darkened gym into the bright hallway.

Buck felt his heart drop into the molten center of the earth.

He had not won her favor after all.

19

BEATRIX

Beatrix sat behind a plastic folding table up on the stage of the biggest hall in the convention and looked out over the audience in the chairs below.

It was a surreal feeling to be part of the group on stage, with a sea of smiling faces observing her.

She'd been down there in the audience so many times.

At the table beside her were some of her heroes - writers, artists, directors and producers of some of the coolest art and films to have been made in the last twenty years.

But somehow she didn't feel the bubbling happiness she had expected at this moment.

She took a sip of the bitter coffee in the paper cup in front of her, hoping she was just tired.

Cecily waved up at her from the audience and Kate grinned and winked. Solo and Kirk were there too.

Only Buck was missing.

And she already knew where he was.

It had been hard to run out the moment his fight was over but she'd had to get here fifteen minutes early for the sound check.

Besides, things weren't going to work out with them anyway.

Kate had pulled her aside this morning to tell her that according to Kirk, Buck had not shown any sign of being romantically interested in Angel or anyone else last night. Kate suspected, though Kirk would not confirm it, that Buck might have only been going to the party to make Bea feel jealous.

But none of that mattered, not really.

Buck wanted privacy.

As she sat at the table, cameras flashing in her eyes every few seconds, Bea knew that if things went the way she wanted them to, privacy was the one thing she couldn't give him.

Maybe not today, maybe not tomorrow, but someday someone would see his picture with her and connect the dots about who and what he really was.

And Bea couldn't live with that.

Though she was beginning to feel like she might not be able to live without him either.

Focus, Bea, her inner mentor told her.

So she turned her smile back on. And when the moderator began asking questions of the panelists, she paid attention to the answers.

"Beatrix Li," the moderator said turning to her at last, with a big smile. "This is your first time up here, isn't it?"

"Yes, this is a pretty amazing feeling," she said. Her newfound confidence allowed her to hold her head high in spite of all those eyes trained on her. "I never realized this room was so big."

The crowd laughed and she felt herself relax. It was okay, they were on her side. She had this.

"We're all fans of *Door to Everywhere*," the moderator said.

There was applause from the crowd.

"Where did you come up with your idea for a portal to another planet?" he went on.

"I think every kid wants to escape," she said carefully. "Whether you're escaping something difficult in your life, or just the everyday struggles of being a teenager. I was a junior in high school when we moved into a mid-century modern apartment building. My closet door had a kind of campy modern look to it that made me think about what might be on the other side if I opened it at just the right moment. I had a cool dream about it one night, and that was the seed for *Door to Everywhere*."

"Very cool," the moderator said.

"I'd always been a fan of Sci-Fi and fantasy," Beatrix went on. "So I wasn't very surprised about where my imagination took me."

Someone in the audience whooped.

"I don't think I've heard this mentioned," the moderator said. "But the planet where Shayla finds herself seems a lot like Aerie, the home planet of the aliens who recently arrived in Stargazer, Pennsylvania."

"That's true," Bea said. "I've often thought the same as I watched the newscasts about those aliens. But of course, *Door to Everywhere* was published long before the aliens in Stargazer came to Earth. So, unless they were sending me signals..."

She trailed off, thinking of things like cosmic destiny and coincidence as the crowd chuckled.

"True," the moderator said. "Well, I guess I'll say what we're all thinking. It's so cool that you're in talks to make *Door to Everywhere* into a film."

The immediate applause and whistles from the audience made Bea smile.

"I can't say too much about the project, since we aren't fully funded quite yet," she said. "But with Kate Henderson and Dirk Malcolm attached, I'm sure we will have all the support we need soon."

She snuck a glance to the center of the table, where Esther Martine sat as the audience applauded their approval of her casting choices.

Esther's snowy white hair was always styled just-so, plus her make-up and jewelry were spot on. She looked like an elderly fashion model.

More importantly though, Esther was a huge investor and she produced with a light touch, allowing artists creative freedom. If Bea could get Esther involved her funding worries would be over.

Bea had hoped they might chat after the panel.

Esther met Bea's eyes, smiled slightly, then looked back to the moderator.

"Well, I think I speak for everyone here when I say that I hope you'll get your funding," he told Bea.

After that he took some questions from the audience for the panel members.

But Bea's mind was racing about the look Esther had given to her.

Could it mean what she hoped?

At last the audience stood to applaud and the panelists waved and followed each other off the stage and into the corridor to the green rooms.

"Beatrix," Esther said in her clear, quiet voice.

"Yes, hi," Bea said breathlessly.

"Walk with me," Esther said.

She walked surprisingly quickly for someone so short.

Bea picked up her pace to keep up with her.

"You need funding for your film," Esther said. "And I've got money and clout. Enough clout not to be bothered by that silly Carson and his smear campaign."

Bea's heart began to pound.

"But I'm not interested," Esther continued. "I didn't want you to think it was Carson, because it isn't. I've got a full docket and a lot of money on the street. And though I liked your book, I think there's a bigger book in you."

Beatrix bit her lip.

Esther stopped walking.

"When you write the next one, call me first," Esther said, pressing a cream-colored business card into Bea's hand. "Don't waste your time with the boys' club."

"Th-thank you," Beatrix said.

"Don't worry, kid, I know I just disappointed you," Esther laughed a dry laugh. "You don't have to pretend to be grateful. But still call me with your next project. I'll make it up to you if it's any good. And I wouldn't have made it as far as I have in this godforsaken business if I didn't keep my word."

It was a better promise than any Bea had gotten from any other investor. She really couldn't complain.

"I appreciate your honesty," Beatrix said.

"Thanks, love," Esther replied, then turned on her heel and marched back toward the convention hall.

Beatrix saw Cecily, Kate, Kirk and Solo nearby, waving at her excitedly from the hallway.

She didn't have the news they all wanted, but she did have good news.

But somehow, it didn't feel like it would be as much fun to share it without Buck there.

20

BUCK

Buck dashed out of the auditorium the moment the battles were completed.

He was still wearing his suit, but he ripped the dollar sign necklace off and stuffed it in his pocket as he ran.

Beatrix's panel was probably over by now, but if there was a chance that he could catch the end of it he didn't mind jogging through the crowds.

On Aerie his hurried movements and muttered apologies for breaking through the crowd would be an unspeakable offense.

But he was beginning to believe that because these humans' days were numbered shorter than those of the citizens of Aerie, they forgave each other's rushing.

He made it to the center of the hall and saw that the stage was empty, except for a couple of teamsters breaking down the table and sound equipment.

He came to a halt.

He had missed it all.

As he stood there, downhearted, a small woman with short white hair and dark blue glasses marched past chattering to the taller, more awkward woman who walked beside her.

The woman with the glasses was Esther Martine, the investor who Beatrix had hoped would make up her funding gap.

"I'm going to pass on it," Esther was saying to her companion as they approached Buck.

"But the graphic novel has such a big following," the other woman said.

Buck's heart sank as he realized that Bea hadn't gotten her funding after all.

"The book was good, but I still don't think it's a blockbuster," Esther said crisply as they passed Buck. "Now *that*. That's going to be the real money maker. I'd fund ten of Beatrix Li's art house projects just to get an exclusive on one of those aliens."

Buck turned to see that Esther Martine was pointing at a booth.

It was a humble table with homemade signs. The proprietors had been at the Philadelphia Comic Con, too.

Their whole booth was dedicated to the aliens back at Stargazer. Blurry photos of Bond, Rocky and Magnum studded the posters hung on the wall behind the table. In spite of all the very beautiful artwork and interesting displays in the convention hall, this modest table was always humming with activity.

Suddenly Esther's words echoed in Buck's head again.

I'd fund ten of Beatrix Li's art house projects to get an exclusive on one of those aliens...

The producer had no idea how close she was to a deal that Beatrix could actually strike.

Or one that Buck could.

If he said he had escaped the Stargazer lab, he could give

that woman the exclusive story she wanted and she could fund Beatrix's project.

It wouldn't make Bea want to be with him.

But at least she would be happy.

He spun around to go after Esther and her friend, and bumped into someone hard.

"Whoa there, buddy," said a familiar voice.

Dirk Malcolm.

"Not you again," Buck said, letting his exasperation get the better of him.

"What's that supposed to mean?" Dirk asked.

"I don't have time to talk," Buck said. "I have to go."

"I'll walk with you," Dirk suggested.

"Suit yourself," Buck replied, heading through the crowd again to try and catch a glimpse of Esther.

Dirk jogged along by his side.

"Who are we trying to catch?" Dirk asked.

"The woman who is supposed to fund your movie," Buck replied.

"I don't think she'd be interested in Bea's project," Dirk said. "She likes blockbusters."

"Well she's going to be interested," Buck said. "I'm going to drop the funding and the girl right in your lap."

"Wait, *what?*" Dirk asked. "Do you think I'm interested in Beatrix?"

"We are men of action," Buck said. "Lies do not become us."

"Man, I'm not lying," Dirk replied. "She's not my type. And besides, she doesn't see me that way. At all."

"She's casting you as the romantic lead, of course she sees you that way," Buck said.

Dirk let out a hearty laugh that stopped Buck in his tracks.

"Dude, I'm playing the *dad,*" Dirk said. "Though I'm flattered that you think I've still got it. Whatever *it* is these days."

Buck studied the man for a second, noting the sincerity in his voice, and the lines around his eyes that certainly hadn't been there in the movie they had watched.

"It's not the age, it's the mileage," Buck replied.

"Tell me about it," Dirk chuckled.

They had made it to the hallway outside the convention hall. Sunlight streamed through the huge glass windows overlooking the Inner Harbor.

"Sit down, buddy, please," Dirk said. "I've got Esther's cell number, for whatever good that will do you. You don't have to chase after her like this."

"This is heavy," Buck said, sinking onto one of the benches overlooking the water.

Dirk sat down beside him.

"Listen," Dirk said after a moment. "I know this is hard for you."

"Please forgive my manners," Buck said. "I don't know what's happening to me."

"It was nothing," Dirk said. "Emotions are a powerful thing. And your frustration is understandable, especially considering who you are, and where you're from."

Buck stole a glance at Dirk. Surely he had misunderstood. The man couldn't know what he was. Beatrix would not have told him.

"You might not know this, but I once played Sherlock Holmes, the famous detective, in a television mini-series," Dirk said. "I'm a method actor. Do you know what that means?"

Buck shook his head.

"It means that I do a lot of research on my characters

and I try to live as them during the duration of a production," Dirk explained. "Not just while they are filming me, but most of the time."

"That sounds... complicated," Buck said.

"Why? We are all playing roles, every moment of every day," Dirk explained. "Right now, I'm trying to play the role of a decent guy who helps out two nice kids. And you're trying to play a regular person instead of a man from another planet."

The reality hit Buck like a punch in the stomach.

"H-how did you know?"

Please don't let Bea have told him. Please don't let her have told him...

"Observation, my dear boy," Dirk said with a pleased grin. "I learned it while playing Holmes. Do you want to know specifics?"

Buck nodded, unable to speak.

"It begins with the handshake," Dirk said.

"I didn't do it properly," Buck chastised himself.

"Not at all," Dirk said. "You have a firm grip and a great shake. But you don't have any calluses. At least not the kind you would have if that body had endured a lifetime of action."

"Oh," said Buck. "That was all?"

"Of course not," Dirk told him. "There are plenty of explanations for the lack of calluses. I saw other things too."

"Like what?" Buck asked.

"Well, for one thing you've quoted three eighties movies since we started this conversation," Dirk said. "And then there's the matter of Beatrix."

"What do you mean?" Buck demanded.

"I mean I've never seen a man look at a woman like

that," Dirk said softly. "You guys have a mate bond, right? It's stronger than anything we have on Earth."

"Oh," Buck said. "Yes. Yes, that's true."

Dirk began to chuckle.

"Why are you laughing?" Buck asked.

"You know I hadn't fully put it together when I had lunch with Bea yesterday," Dirk replied. "No wonder she looked shaken when I told her to aim for the stars."

Buck merely stared at him, wondering how soon his secrets would be spilled.

"You don't need to worry," Dirk said. "I won't tell anyone. I just thought it might help you to know that I already knew."

"I need your help," Buck heard himself say to the other man.

"What do you need?" Dirk asked.

"I need advice," Buck said. "I overheard Esther Martine say that she would be willing to fund ten art house movies if she could get her hands on an exclusive from an alien."

"That sounds like something she would say," Dirk said fondly.

"So, I'm thinking of offering her my story," Buck said. "In exchange for funding Bea's movie."

"Yeah, that'll work," Dirk said, nodding vigorously. "But are you sure Beatrix would want you to do that? She strikes me as the kind of person who likes to fight her own battles."

"She is," Buck agreed. "But I'll be damned if I won't help give her a fighting chance."

"Fair enough," Dirk agreed, slipping his phone out of his pocket.

He jotted down a number on a card with his own face and handed it over to Buck.

"That's Esther's number," he said. "Just don't call her

until you're one hundred percent serious. That woman means business. I wrote down the number of a big blogger too - you might mention what's going on to both sources at once - get you bigger results. Do you have a cell phone?"

Buck shook his head.

"Take my spare," Dirk said, offering him a phone. "Just don't use it to phone home."

Dirk winked.

"Thank you, Dirk Malcolm," Buck told him with feeling.

"Don't mention it, kid," Dirk said, patting him on the back. "Take care of yourself."

Buck watched as the older man strode down the hallway.

Then he closed his eyes and reached out to his brother, Bond. Before he made any calls, he needed Bond's blessing.

Though a great many miles separated the two of them, he could feel the stirring of Bond's mind inside his at once, like sand shifting in an hour glass.

I know the only thing you asked of me was to hide myself, Buck began. *But I love her. And she needs this.*

21

BEATRIX

Beatrix walked down the hallway with her friends, trying not to scour the crowd for Buck, and failing.

Solo must have noticed her eyes scanning the faces.

"Buck is still at his tournament," he told her softly. "He wanted to see your panel. But the tournament must not have finished in time."

"Thanks," she said, not bothering to deny that she had been looking for Buck.

Solo gave her a sad smile.

Bea wondered what was happening with him and Cecily. Kate and Kirk had obviously been destined for each other, and though Bea and Buck might be more star-crossed than fated, the attraction was certainly there.

But Solo and Cecily seemed to have a sturdy friendship, with no sign of romance at all. She wasn't sure if that was mutual or if Cecily was keeping the big alien at arm's length on purpose.

"Hey, writer-lady," Dirk Malcolm called to her from across the corridor. "I guess congratulations are in order."

"I need to talk to him, guys," Beatrix muttered.

Cecily nodded to her and the group walked on.

She jogged over to Dirk, shaking her head.

"I heard about the *real alien* thing," Dirk said before she could explain about Esther. "I think it's great and I'm totally onboard."

"What?" Bea asked.

"Buck told me," Dirk said. "Man does he care about you. He's making the calls now so you might want to be ready."

"What calls?" Bea asked.

"You know, to Esther Martine. I suggested he reach out to a blogger friend of mine as well, just to get a little buzz going," Dirk said. "Martine's going to flip at the chance to get an exclusive with a real alien. There's no chance she won't fund your movie now."

The truth descended on Bea at once and she felt the air go out of her lungs with a whoosh.

Her feet began moving before her brain had fully processed what was happening.

She had to get to Buck, to stop him. He was sacrificing everything.

"Hey, where are you going?" Dirk yelled after her. "Just to be clear, whatever his exclusive is, I want to be in it."

But Beatrix was already running faster, her shoes beating a breathless tattoo against the carpet of the corridor. Dirk had just seen Buck and he had come from this direction.

Dirk's words echoed in her head.

Man, does he care about you...

And he did - he clearly did. Buck's actions spoke louder than words.

The only problem was that she cared about him, too.

She would never want him to give up what mattered to him just to bring her career success.

If today had taught her anything it was that without him, her career success or failure didn't seem to matter much.

But if she didn't catch him now, it would be too late.

A moment later she saw his big form silhouetted against the late afternoon sun coming in the big plate glass window.

Buck leaned against the glass on one arm, his other hand in his pocket. The suit made him look like the cover of a billionaire romance novel. Bea would have giggled at the idea, if she hadn't been so relieved to find him.

"Buck," she called out.

His brown eyes met hers and he smiled warmly.

"Oh, thank god I caught you," she sighed. "Please don't call Martine or that other person. I don't want her money. I'll find another way."

Buck's face fell.

"What is it?" she asked.

"Oh, Beatrix," he said. "I already called. I'm meeting the blogger and a photographer in a few minutes."

"Come on," Beatrix said, grabbing his arm and tugging with a strength she didn't know she had.

"Where are we going?" Buck asked as they burst into the crowd again.

"To the green room, to figure out how to undo this," she told him.

"But, Bea," he began.

"No," she told him as they jogged between the convention-goers. "This is not happening on my watch."

22

BEATRIX

Beatrix slammed the green room door shut behind her and locked it.

Then she spun around to fix Buck in her gaze.

Out of the corner of her eye she could see Kate, Kirk, Cecily and Solo seated at the mirrors. It was typical for them to hang out in here with her.

But they were about to get quite a show.

Because there was no way she could bottle up what she was about to say to Buck.

"How could you do this?" she demanded.

"I was trying to help you," he replied calmly.

"I don't need your help," she wailed.

"That's true," he agreed. "You are a strong, capable woman. You don't need anyone's help. But I want to help you anyway."

"Why?" she asked, though she knew the answer. He had been telling it to her every way he knew how since the moment they'd met.

"Because I love you," he told her. "And because if I can help you fulfill your destiny by sharing that beautiful book with a generation of Earth's young people, then any sacrifice would be worthwhile."

There was a knock on the door.

Beatrix ignored it.

She gazed up into the fathomless depths of Buck's dark eyes.

She had no idea what his life had been like on Aerie, no idea what he had held dear.

But here he was, so new to this world, with no doubt, no fear in his heart.

It was no wonder her own fears had begun to dissolve. His zest for living in the moment was infectious.

Bea had spent a lifetime balancing on a tightrope between fear and hope.

Now it was time to dive for the nets.

"Guys," Cecily said from the door. Her eye was to the peephole.

"Not now," Bea said.

"But—" Cecily began.

"Buck, I've spent my life afraid that I wouldn't do things the right way," Bea said. "But that ends now. I'm not letting you reveal yourself. If I can't make the movie I'll just write another book. All I care about is you."

"Bea," Buck breathed.

Suddenly the room seemed so small and his big presence so immediate. The air between them sizzled and Beatrix felt herself melting with a need for him to claim her.

"*Guys,*" Cecily said. "There are reporters out there *right now.*"

"Shit," Kate said.

"Just one blogger, right?" Buck asked.

Cecily shook her head. "He must have owed a bunch of

'someones' a favor, because there are probably a dozen reporters with camera crews out there."

"We'll just stay in here," Bea shrugged.

There was another knock on the door.

"There's no back way out," Kate said.

"But all three of you are here," Beatrix realized looking at the alien brothers. "How can we possibly play this off as nothing when they see all of you at once?"

"Buck," Kirk said, handing his brother an eyeliner pencil from the dressing table.

"Really, brother?" Buck asked.

"Now or never," Kirk shrugged. "And she loves you."

Buck looked appraisingly at Beatrix.

"What?" she asked, mystified.

Instead of answering, Buck walked over to the wall opposite the door.

There was only a tiny transom window close to ceiling height there. It was far too small for a person to fit through.

But Buck squatted in front of the wall, extended the eyeliner out in front of him and began to press it to the drywall.

Bea watched as he sketched a straight line up over his head.

"We know you're in there," someone shouted through the green room door.

Buck ignored it and swept the line over in an arc, then brought it down to the floor again on the other side.

It looked like... a door.

He stepped back to look at it, then, apparently satisfied with his work, he drew a circle on the right side of it.

A knob.

And before Bea's eyes, it seemed to *expand* into three

dimensions - the black circle sliding outward into an ivory white knob with a black plate attaching it to the white door.

"Is that...?" Bea whispered, but she couldn't finish her sentence.

Buck was drawing hinges on the opposite side.

He straightened, turned and looked into her eyes.

"I'm sorry I didn't get to talk to you about this before showing you," he said. "I hope you're not frightened."

She shook her head slowly.

He smiled, grasped the knob, and turned the handle.

A rush of hot city air burst into the room. It smelled like exhaust and the hotdog vendor's cart.

Buck gestured for Bea to exit and they stepped out onto the sidewalk together.

23

BUCK

Buck stood on the city sidewalk, looking down at Beatrix, trying to read the expression on her beautiful face.

The summer breeze swirled around them, lifting her hair in inky ribbons. But the rest of her was stone still, shoulders squared.

Behind her, the others stepped through the door and joined them on the street.

"Are you okay?" Buck asked.

"Let's go home," Beatrix said. "I need to talk with you. Alone."

"Um, we we're going to grab some dinner," Solo said.

"No we're not," Cecily said. "We're going to fix things with Dirk's blogger. Come on."

She shot Buck and Beatrix a confident wink as she turned to head back inside. He didn't know what she had in mind, but she seemed like she had it under control.

That was good. Buck's mind was too full of Beatrix to be much help in planning.

The others trailed off toward the main entrance of the convention center, leaving Buck alone with Beatrix.

Bea began to march down the street toward their rental. She seemed to be moving awfully quickly on those short legs of hers.

Buck jogged to keep up.

"I'm sorry I didn't tell you before," he told her. "Dr. Bhimani said we shouldn't share our gifts until we were mated. She said it might frighten you away."

Beatrix stopped her march.

"Do I seem frightened?" she asked.

"Well... no," Buck said. "You seem, um, determined."

"I am determined," she told him with a half smile.

Then she turned and marched on.

Buck's heart lifted as he began to understand that the reason for her pace might just be urgency, rather than fear or anger.

They had reached the lobby of the building now.

Beatrix walked briskly through the doors and pressed the button to call the elevator.

The doors slid open immediately.

They both stepped in.

It wasn't until the doors closed again that it hit him that they were alone.

Bea gazed at him like a hungry tiger.

Buck's instincts took over. He slammed his hands against the walls of the elevator on either side of her and leaned in to take the kiss that he knew she wanted to give.

But at the last second he restrained himself.

He had to know.

"Why?" he asked as gently as he could, sliding one of his hands from the wall behind her to caress her cheek.

"Why what?" she whispered, her eyes on his lips.

"You didn't want this before," he said. "You must have had your reasons. Why don't they matter anymore? Will they matter again tomorrow?"

She looked up into his eyes for a moment.

"I had a million reasons," she said. "I've never had a serious relationship and you want a mate for life. My career is taking off and falling in love is a complication. You want privacy and one day I may become a very public person. There are countless reasons why this doesn't fit what I thought I wanted."

"So, this is a mistake then," Buck murmured, unable for the life of him, to remove his hand from her soft cheek.

"No," she smiled up at him. "What I thought I wanted was the mistake. There's not one part of my life plan that wouldn't be better with you in it."

"But your movie," he said.

"You know I've been thinking about it since my talk with Esther, and I had it all wrong," she said. "*Door to Everywhere* is kind of a cult favorite. It has an indie following but it never hit a bestseller list. It was a small budget book. Hell, I couldn't even afford color panels."

"It's a wonderful book," Buck said.

"I think its humble presentation may have something to do with that," Bea said slowly. "Esther Martine's been doing this a long time. If she doesn't sense a blockbuster I trust her instincts."

"*Door to Everywhere* will make a great movie," Buck said, furious that one person's opinion could influence Bea's sense of confidence.

"Oh, it will definitely be a great movie," Bea smiled up at him. "But it's going to be a small budget indie film, not a big studio production. If I lose my funders over that, it's fine by me. I'll come up with the money we need and we'll do it on a shoestring. But I'll do it my way. The story will come first, it will not be outshone."

"Are you really okay with that?" Buck asked.

"I feel the same anticipation I did when I wrote it," Bea said with a smile. "And this is the first time I've felt that, since the talks of an adaption started."

He could sense that she was telling the truth. The air was practically humming with her happiness.

He leaned in again to give her the kiss they both longed for.

But the ding of the elevator interrupted them.

He took her by the hand instead and led her out of the elevator to the door of the condo.

She slipped the key out of her pocket and opened it.

The last of the afternoon's pink sunset filtered through the curtains. It was enough to show them the way to her room.

Beatrix smiled when she reached her door.

"Why are you smiling?" he asked her, charmed by the curve of her lips.

"I was thinking of my door to everywhere," she said. "And how it always leads to you."

Overcome with emotion, he swept her into his arms, closed the door behind them and placed her gently on the bed.

She looked up at him, her eyes luminous.

"Do you want to sleep on this?" he asked her.

"No," she said, smiling, her hands dancing down the buttons on the front of her dress.

"By the moons of Aerie," he murmured, mesmerized.

"Aren't you going to undress too?" she asked him.

He turned from her, peeled his t-shirt over his head, took off his shoes and socks, then unbuttoned his jeans and slid them off, taking the boxers with them.

When he turned back she was naked, her dark hair spread across the pillow, arms outstretched to him.

He paused for just a moment, trying to memorize the glow of her skin in the twilight, the longing in her dark eyes.

Then he could restrain himself no more.

He crawled on top of her, pinning her to the bed with his hips, resting on one elbow and sliding his hand into the silk of her hair.

"Bea," he crooned. "You are so beautiful."

"Thank you," she smiled up at him. "You're not bad yourself."

Then she looked downward, eyelashes kissing her cheeks.

"Don't you dare do that," he told her. "Don't be shy with me."

He kissed her eyelids and she giggled.

"Are you giggling at me?" he demanded playfully.

She shook her head but her eyes were dancing.

"Now you will be punished," he informed her.

Her eyes widened.

Quick as a thought, he pinned her hands over her head and lowered his face to hers.

"I'm going to have my way with you now," he whispered. "Is that okay with you?"

She smiled.

"I need to hear you say it, my mate," he told her.

"Yes," she whispered.

A wave of lust surged in his veins, but he fought it back.

"Nice," he praised her and brushed his lips lightly against hers.

She seemed to melt under him.

He kissed her again, pressing his lips firmly against hers this time.

She kissed him back parting her lips slightly as if in invitation.

But he was already nuzzling her jaw, burying his face in her neck and feasting on the tender flesh where it met her shoulder.

Bea inhaled and angled her head to give him better access.

Her utter submission was exciting him wildly. His body, which he had kept so firmly under control, ached and roared with need.

Bea whimpered as he trailed kisses down her chest.

"I'm going to let go of your hands now," he told her, his own voice a raspy growl he hardly recognized. "But you're going to leave them right where they are."

"Yes," she whispered.

He pulled back and looked down at her, arms twined above her head, her face flushed, breasts heaving, the dusky nipples pouting, begging for his touch.

He fell on her, licking and nipping at one breast as she made sweet sounds of pleasure, then abandoning it to tease and torment the other as he grazed the first with his thumb.

When her hips began to tremble, he gave each breast one last kiss, then made his way down past her belly to the apex of her thighs.

Beatrix was panting now, her eyes wide as she watched him position himself between her legs.

She knew what was next - he had done this to her before.

But she still cried out the moment his tongue touched her.

She tasted like honey and he lapped at her frantically.

Beatrix whimpered and lifted her hips to meet his mouth, angling herself as if desperate for his tongue to caress her stiff little clitoris.

He responded with long, slow strokes of his tongue against her opening, teasing her with a feather light touch where she most wanted firmness, prolonging the anticipation for what they both knew was coming.

He had just begun to ease a finger inside her when she began to beg.

"Please," she moaned plaintively, her sex swelling against his tongue.

His own corresponding wave of desire stiffened his cock to the point of pain.

"Oh my love," he whispered to her, crawling back up to cradle her head in his arms. "I will take care of you. I will give you what you need."

She pressed her lips to his, bringing her arms down to twine around his neck.

"Beatrix Li," he whispered to her. "I choose you as my mate. Will you accept me?"

"I accept you," she whispered back with shining eyes.

Buck's heart was filled to bursting.

"Are you ready, my angel?" he asked her.

She nodded.

He took his bursting cock in his hand and guided it against her.

The satiny hot feel of her against the tip of his rigid penis was almost enough to send him over the edge. He gritted his teeth against the pleasure and pressed himself slowly inside her.

At last he filled her completely. The feeling was so heavenly he felt almost unmoored from reality.

He looked down at her beautiful face to anchor himself, and prayed for the strength to make this good for her, as perfect as she deserved.

24

BEATRIX

Beatrix looked up at the man of her dreams. His handsome face was suffused with pleasure and she felt a rush of happiness knowing that it was her body transporting him.

Then he moved inside her and all thought was lost to the sensation.

She had done this before, but that had been like a sketch compared to this masterpiece.

He filled her again and she felt it in every cell of her body, as if tiny bubbles were rising in her, effervescent.

He groaned when he pulled himself out of her again, and gasped with pleasure at the next thrust.

Beatrix lifted her hips to urge him on, sinking her nails into his shoulders.

He slammed into her faster now as if electrified by her rough touch.

The pleasure was almost unbearable, Beatrix lost track of her own sounds as her ecstasy coiled up inside her tighter and tighter, ready to burst.

Buck slid a big hand between them and drew gentle circles on her throbbing clitoris.

"Ohhhh," Beatrix cried as he drove into her again.

And then the room half faded away as he ignited her like a firework with his clever fingers.

Bea was flying, flying and then the pleasure crashed down on her, sending her rocketing back to earth in endless waves of rapture.

"Oh, god, Bea," he groaned.

She felt him swell impossibly inside her and then jet inside her again and again, as if in harmony with her own surges of pleasure.

A sudden stillness filled the air.

Then she felt as if a cool breeze had kissed her heated cheeks, though the windows were closed.

Buck rested his head on her chest and she moved her hands into his hair, cradling him against her as she imagined she might one day cradle the child they would have together. A child they might have just conceived.

Strangely, the thought didn't worry her. It felt like the most natural thing in the world.

She was just beginning to drift off when she felt slight movement in the air again.

She opened her eyes.

A butterfly had alighted on the table next to the bed. It paused there, lacy wings trembling delicately.

"Buck," she whispered. "Look."

"That looks like..." he trailed off, but she already knew what he had been about to say.

It looked like one of the butterflies she had been drawing.

Movement in her periphery made her turn her head.

One of her paper drawings tacked to the wall was flapping in the breeze.

No.

There was no breeze.

The drawing *on* the paper flapped and stretched its gauzy wings, then fluttered off the page

Then another and another of her butterflies flickered off the papers she had absentmindedly sketched them on since the night of her dream.

Their wings were soft purples and blues in the moonlight, delicate as lace, vibrant as a technicolor movie.

"Did you do that?" she breathed.

He shook his head.

"Then how...?"

"*You* did it, Bea," he told her. "They are yours, you brought them to life."

She stared at him, unable to comprehend.

"Dr. Bhimani said this happens sometimes too," he explained. "At the moment of our mating I shared my gift with you."

"Your gift," she echoed.

"Yes," he told her. "Are you scared?"

She shook her head and smiled. "No, but I'm pretty sure I must be dreaming," she confided in him.

"Only one way to find out," he told her.

She gazed up at him in question.

He answered by pressing her lips with his in an unhurried kiss that was rich with promise.

"Slowly this time," he told her as a butterfly landed in his hair. "We wouldn't want to scare away your new pets..."

25

CECILY

Cecily handed her satchel over to Kate as they marched back into the convention hall.

"Put it on as fast as you can, over your clothes," she told Kate.

"It's heavy," Kate remarked.

"I'm going to stall them for as long as I can, but that might not be long," Cecily continued. "If Dirk's source is who I think it is, he's going to be pretty pissed."

"What *is* this?" Kate asked, peeking into the bag.

"It's the Night Bird," Cecily said.

"What?" Kate asked, stopping mid-step. "That's not possible. It would have to be done in CG."

"Keep walking," Cecily said. "It is possible. At least I think it is. We're about to find out. Give me your key."

They had reached the corridor leading to the green room. Kate slid the key out of her pocket and handed it to Cecily.

Ahead of them, reporters and bloggers clogged the hall.

Cecily almost felt sorry for them. She hoped she could make the trip worth their while.

She turned to Solo and Kirk who were trailing them.

"Guys, you can't be with us when they're looking for aliens," she said. "Can you run downstairs to the cafe and wait for us?"

Kirk looked pained, but Solo stepped forward.

"Of course we can, Cecily," he said. "If you are sure you have no need for our assistance here."

She looked up at his unbelievably gorgeous face. He was always so confident, so calm. It was charming and all, but secretly Cecily wondered when his facade would break. Surely no one could be so patient and so smooth forever.

He had been nothing but a good friend to her, so she felt perverse wishing for the straw that would break the camel's back.

But if experience had taught her anything, it was that people, and men in particular, were the opposite of steady and polite.

Sooner or later that handsome veneer would crack and Cecily would see what Solo was really made of.

But that day was not today.

"I'm sure," she said. "We're fine."

He nodded and took Kirk by the arm, leading him back into the convention hall.

"Are you ready for this?" Cecily asked, turning to Kate.

"Does it matter?" Kate asked, arching an eyebrow.

"Not really," Cecily said. "But it will be fun. When we get to the door I'll open it and you'll go in, ostensibly to look for Bea."

Kate nodded and they headed into the crowd.

"Hey, fellas," Cecily called out.

"Cecily Page," one of the bloggers called happily to her. She recognized him as a kid she'd given quotes to after she'd done costumes on Jocelyn Wylde's latest music video.

"Do you know where Beatrix Li is?" another reporter demanded, sounding less happy.

"Cool your jets," she advised lightly. "I'm going in there to look for her."

A narrow pathway opened up for her and she dragged Kate behind her.

She opened the door and Kate slipped in.

A woman with a mohawk and a digital recorder tried to follow.

"No, no, no," Cecily said, blocking her. "The green room is private space. Let me see if Bea texted me."

She slid her cell phone out of her pocket and pretended to check her text messages.

She was really pulling up an app that she prayed would work. She'd fooled around with a single scale and even a whole glove once. Hopefully it would work on a larger canvas.

"Is Bea in there?" she called to Kate through the door.

"No," Kate said.

There were groans from the crowd and Cecily saw one or two people already heading away back down the corridor.

"You know what? You guys came all the way out here," she said. "You want to see my newest project?"

There were smiles and nods. One of the guys who was leaving stopped and turned around, but didn't walk back.

"Kate, come out here," she called through the door. "Let's show these lucky bastards this costume for the first time. Move back guys, give her some space."

She waited until they had backed up significantly. The green room was opposite a part of the corridor that opened up into a sort of open lobby with a huge picture window, some sofas and assorted potted trees and plants as well as some framed modern artwork. It was as near to perfect for this stunt as could be even if she'd had time to plan. Which she hadn't.

"Okay, ladies and gentlemen, I present to you, the Night Bird," she called out.

The door opened and Kate slipped out.

Cecily looked out at the reporters, they were watching, a few murmuring to each other.

The Night Bird in *Door to Everywhere* was a shifting Cheshire Cat of a character, appearing out of nowhere and disappearing again into the night.

Cecily had been fascinated with the idea of making a Night Bird costume. And then a documentary about the clever camouflage of the cuttlefish gave her the spark of inspiration she needed to actually be able to pull it off.

Kate stepped into the lobby area in the full costume, tiny scales shimmering all over her body.

She stood and faced the gathered crowd, her back to the chocolate brown wall.

Cecily held up a finger and Kate nodded.

Cecily's fingers danced on the screen of the phone.

"Ladies and gentlemen," Cecily announced. "Here is your alien."

Suddenly Kate's body seemed to almost disappear into the wall behind her.

There were sounds of surprise from the bloggers and reporters. A wall of cell phones was raised to record.

"What is that?" one reporter asked.

"This suit is made up of scales, each of which is an LED," Cecily explained. "I can control each scale using an app on my phone."

She nodded to Kate, who moved across the sitting area

to stand in front of the green accent wall with a painting of a red circle above the cream colored chair rail.

Cecily swiped and tapped and suddenly Kate's lower half was green with a cream colored belt and her torso was emblazoned with the portion of the red circle it covered.

"Jesus," one of the bloggers whispered.

"That's - that's military level tech," another one stammered.

"It was supposed to be," Cecily agreed. "This batch of tiny LEDs was rejected for government experimental use due to minor imperfections. I bought them at auction and encased them in transparent scales that I poured from a hand carved mold. I think they're good enough for the movies. What do you guys think?"

A burst of impromptu applause broke out.

Cecily grinned, feeling really pleased.

Kate bowed and Cecily managed to swipe the phone fast enough to turn her friend completely green and then back to belted and spotted as she straightened.

"Does this mean the funding is in place for *Door to Everywhere* to be made?" one reporter asked.

"It's in the works," Cecily agreed. "You guys might be able to help us out with that if you spread this around."

There was laughter, followed by a smattering of applause that picked up when Kate sat on the blue and beige striped sofa and Cecily managed to make her blend into it.

"Thanks for coming out to see this first," Cecily called to the crowd. "You guys are the best. But we've got to get going, the suit needs to be recharged."

Kate hopped up and came to her as the crowd began to dissipate.

"This is amazing," Kate said, wide-eyed.

"Thanks," Cecily replied. "I'm just glad it worked."

They had almost reached the green room door when a blogger grabbed Cecily's elbow.

She turned to see Ed Corland, Dirk's blogger contact. Ed was a pretty big name. He was one of the older bloggers that had survived the transition from print journalism.

"Hey, this isn't cool," Ed told Cecily.

"I'd like to see you make a better invisibility suit," Kate retorted, pretending not to understand.

"Funny," he said to Kate, then turned back to Cecily. "I mean it's not cool that you say you've got Stargazer aliens and you really have some dumb PR stunt. Again."

"Sorry about that," Cecily said. "But I hope you can use the footage."

"Next time, just be honest with us," Ed said. "You've got some cool effects. This thing's really neat. And I don't know how you pulled that crap in Philly with the piano but I hauled ass up there for aliens and I wasn't sorry when I saw it. I just don't like being lied to."

"Point taken," Cecily said. "Next time I'll let you know what's really going on, Ed."

"Appreciate it," he said, tipping his baseball cap. "Good luck with your movie, kids."

He headed off down the corridor after the others.

"Are you okay?" Kate asked Cecily.

"I'm fine," Cecily said. "And thank you - you were great."

"I guess we should get out of here," Kate said. "I'm ready to go back to the rental for wine and pizza."

"Not so fast," Cecily chuckled. "I think Bea and Buck probably need a little privacy."

"Do you really think so?" she asked.

"Did you see Bea's face?" Cecily asked.

"I wasn't sure if she was mad at him," Kate said.

"Oh, you would have known if she was mad," Cecily said, raising her eyebrows.

"Holy cow," Kate said. "That's awesome. I'm so happy for them."

"Me too," Cecily said.

"So..."

"So what?" Cecily pretended not to understand and prayed for a distraction, *any* distraction, to get them off this topic.

"It seems like Solo really likes you," Kate said slowly.

"He's a nice guy," Cecily agreed lightly. "Let's get you out of that costume. I'll bet those scales are getting heavy."

To her credit, Kate nodded and didn't press for more.

As they headed into the green room to remove the suit, Cecily found that she was actually feeling quite eager to meet up with the boys downstairs and tell them all that had happened.

Though her heart pounded at the idea of sharing her big moment with Solo, she convinced herself that telling Kirk what had happened was just as big a part of the fun.

After all, Cecily had no intention of getting involved with Solo. He was just a friend.

Just a big, sexy, loyal friend...

26

BUCK

Buck fought valiantly, his hair wet with sweat as the crowd below him cheered.

Somehow in today's tournament he had survived his first fight with Alex. He suspected that Alex might have let him win because Beatrix was in the front row.

But winning the first match, and his opponent's unexpected withdrawal from his next match, meant he was now fighting Angel for the title.

He had learned that the audience enjoyed when the gladiators pretended to be angry with each other, so he glowered at Angel and pretended to snarl.

She fixed him with an icy gaze, and flexed her mighty arms.

He really didn't have a chance.

But he hoped to the stars that somehow he would get lucky and win anyway.

Though he knew he and Beatrix were joined forever in their mate bond, he hadn't asked her the practical and very human question that burned in his heart.

He and Angel bowed to each other. Her pink hair slid

over the wing tattoos on her shoulders as she straightened up.

She thrust first, as he expected she would. Her weapon had a harp shaped handle covered in a brilliant metallic sheen that shimmered in the stage lights as she moved.

Buck managed to duck under her reach.

She thrust again, so he blocked, then slid his own weapon forward, trying to disarm her.

"Not on my watch, pretty boy," Angel shouted and leapt.

At first he didn't realize what she was doing.

And by the time he did, it was too late.

His opponent landed hard on the edge of his platform, sending him soaring into the air like a pancake being flipped.

It was a move the other gladiators called the Holy Grail, though Buck could not understand how it related to King Arthur.

At any rate, it was epic, and everyone would be delighted. If he had to lose the tournament, this was an excellent way to go out.

Everything seemed to slow down as Buck sailed off the platform and curved sideways through the air.

The gasps of the crowd stretched out and he felt as if he were floating.

He came to rest on the sand floor of the stage, his hip and shoulder absorbing most of the impact.

There was a moment of utter silence.

He leapt hurriedly to his feet, arms lifted to show that he was okay.

The crowd went wild.

Angel grinned widely and threw him a kiss.

Buck waved at her. She really was the best gladiator.

Then he looked for Bea in the crowd.

She shook her head, eyes sparkling, looking very relieved.

"And our title goes to Angel. That was quite a match, little lady," the announcer crowed into the microphone, walking over to hold it up to Angel.

"I don't think anyone's ever called me little lady before," Angel teased.

"What would you like to be called?" the announcer asked, looking worried.

"Just Angel is fine by me," she said, grinning.

"To the victor go the spoils," the announcer said. "Whose favor were you fighting for today?"

"His," she said loudly and clearly, pointing to someone in the audience.

Everyone turned en masse.

The spotlight operator obligingly aimed the light at someone who looked very familiar.

That someone pulled off his sunglasses and baseball cap.

"Dirk Malcolm," the announcer said in a surprised way. "It's an honor to have you here, sir."

"It's a pleasure to be here," Dirk called back.

The audience began to make excited noises.

"Well, the lady fought for your honor," the announcer said, smiling. "What do you say?"

"I say she rocked my world," Dirk said, nodding.

"Not as much as she rocked his," the announcer pointed out, indicating Buck.

The audience laughed and Buck smiled and nodded.

"Does she have your favor?" the announcer asked Dirk.

"She certainly does," he said, looking straight at Angel with unmistakable interest.

Angel's cheeks flushed as pink as her hair and for once

she had no comeback, though the announcer put the mic to her mouth.

"There you have it, ladies and gentlemen," the announcer said. "T-shirts are on sale at the table in the corridor. Thanks for coming!"

The crowd began to disperse, though Dirk Malcolm was picking his way through it to get to Angel.

Beatrix came to Buck too, climbing onto the stage to join him.

"Hey," she said. "Are you okay?"

"I'm fine," he said. "She's really good."

"She's been training a long time," Bea said. "So you can't let it get you down."

"Of course not," Buck agreed. "I was just really hoping to win."

"Why?" Bea asked.

"Well, this tournament was to win favor, but traditional gladiator battles were done to win a lady's hand in marriage," Buck said slowly.

"But I don't need you to fight a gladiator battle to win my hand away from my father," Beatrix said. "I'm a free woman. I can marry the man I want, whether he pushed someone off a platform or not."

And Buck smiled as he realized that he might have a pretty good shot at winning Bea's hand today after all.

So he knelt in the sand of the stage and pulled the ring from his pocket.

It was small and very dainty. He had bought it from an elf at the convention. At least she had looked like an elf, but buck knew it was probably a costume.

The ring itself was made of tiny golden willow branches. He hoped they would remind Beatrix of the tree in her book. One day he would replace it with something magnificent, heavy with diamonds. But today, he hoped it would be enough.

"Beatrix Li, will you marry me?" he asked.

"I agreed to be bound to you forever last night," she said in wonder. "Is this really necessary?"

"That was an Aerie tradition," he said quietly, so that only she would hear him. "This is an Earth tradition. It is important to your people - to our people," he corrected himself. "But only if you are ready. Are you ready?"

"Yes," she shouted, her voice carrying throughout the hall. "Yes, of course I will marry you."

The crowd broke into applause as he slid the ring onto her finger.

But Buck only had eyes for his mate's beautiful smile.

27

BEATRIX

Beatrix walked with Buck down the corridor to the convention hall to retrieve her backpack.

Somehow everything looked brighter today - the sunlight pouring through the windows overlooking the Inner Harbor was more brilliant than it had been the day before. The abstract paintings on the walls looked more like ripe tomatoes than murder scenes. Even the sounds of the visitors leaving the con were happier and less tired.

And Beatrix herself felt light as air, as if she could take a running leap and actually fly, like one of the butterflies she'd drawn.

"What is making you smile, my mate?" Buck asked.

His rough voice sent fingers of anticipation down her spine.

"I'm just... happy," she told him, looking down at the slim gold band around her finger. The tiny golden willow branches were exactly what she had pictured when she wrote that scene in *Door to Everywhere*.

"Me too," he said.

He wrapped her hand in his and pulled it to his mouth, placing a gentle kiss on her ring finger.

"So what now?" Buck asked.

"I guess we find the others and go back to the rental and pack," she told him. "We're going to drive all the way out to the Glacier City Comic Con, so we'll have to leave soon."

"Would we not take an aircraft if Glacier City is so far away?" Buck asked.

"It's not easy to travel by air without identification," Bea explained carefully. "Besides, who doesn't love a road trip?"

"The road trip is a proud human tradition," Buck said solemnly.

Beatrix found herself laughing. She had so much to show him, and she fully expected to fall in love with the world all over again as she saw it through Buck's fresh eyes.

They were nearly at her table when she noticed a woman standing inside the rope enclosure. She was average height with a sea of onyx braids brushing the shoulders of what looked like a very expensive suit.

"Beatrix Li?" the woman asked, turning around.

As she turned, a girl stepped out from where she had been hidden behind her mother. It was the pre-teen with homemade cartoons on her canvas sneakers. She had attended nearly every one of Bea's sessions. Bea had developed a real soft spot for her.

"Hi there," Bea said. "I'm really sorry, but the convention is over. We're supposed to be cleaning our stuff out now."

"Oh, don't worry about that. I'm with Jensen BioTech. We're one of the sponsors. Marjorie Anderson," the woman said, extending her hand.

"Nice to meet you, Mrs. Anderson," Bea replied, shaking it. She'd heard of Jensen BioTech - they were all over the news with their recent development of a way to electronically upload and store human memories.

"Just Marjorie," the woman smiled.

"And this is my... fiancé, Buck," Bea explained, thinking how funny it was to use the word for the first time with a complete stranger.

"Great to meet you, Buck," Marjorie said. "And maybe you two remember my daughter, Hailey?"

"Of course," Beatrix said. "It's good to see you again, Hailey."

Hailey nodded coolly.

Beatrix gave herself an internal high five. In pre-teen, a cool nod was the equivalent of a bear hug.

"What can we do for you guys?" Beatrix asked.

"Well that's just it," Marjorie said. "You've already done it. Hailey really enjoyed the convention, and that's thanks to your efforts. I know she'll roll her eyes, but I've missed seeing a smile on my daughter's face. And she's been so passionate and excited about the approach to art that you taught her, and the big-hearted way you worked with her and with the other kids. I understand you're as introverted as she is, so I know it was no small effort for you to extend your gift to others. Now we're here to find out what we can do for you."

Beatrix opened her mouth and closed it again, unsure what the woman wanted her to say.

"Let me make it easy for you," Marjorie said with a warm smile. "Hailey did a bit of digging on social media. We read that you lost funding for your movie because one of your actors was sexually harassed by the son of a producer."

"Oh," Bea said. She knew the professional thing to do was sidestep the issue, but she had never had a fan address it head on in person like this. "I'm going to be fine, Marjorie.

We've had a recent, um, breakthrough in our animation technique. And I think we can do the story very well as a small indie film. We're just planning to regroup on the timing and the scale of the project."

"I make it a point to instill in my daughter that standing up to bullies is important," Marjorie went on. "But I find that showing her what I believe in is more effective than telling her. So with that in mind, I'm prepared to invest in your project to whatever extent you need my help. I don't care if the movie is big or small, that's not really my field. You just tell me how much and I'll write the check."

"Wow, that's very generous," Beatrix said, tears prickling her eyes. She knew the average person couldn't actually cover the difference between what she had and what she would need, but she was incredibly moved.

"It's not generous at all," Marjorie said. "It's very savvy on my part because I know how that book spoke to my child, and I imagine I'll do quite well with this investment."

She slid a card out of a golden case and handed it to Beatrix.

"Email me with a rundown of exactly what you have and what you need, and how else I can help you," Marjorie said.

Beatrix looked down at the card. It had the gold leaf logo of Jensen BioTech. Underneath it said:

MARJORIE ANDERSON - FOUNDER/CEO

THE WORDS BEGAN to swim in front of her eyes.

This woman wasn't some random employee or executive. She was the head of one of the hottest BioTech compa-

nies in the world. She could fund every movie Beatrix
ever made.

"I named the company after my mentor, Arthur Jensen,"
Marjorie said. "One day I'll tell you the story of how he
helped me, because he saw a spark in me, just like what my
daughter sees in you."

"I- I don't know what to say," Beatrix stammered.

"Don't say anything, but do shoot me an email as soon as
you have a minute," Marjorie laughed. "Come on, Hailey,
let's get out of the way so these two can pack up. Are you
happy, kiddo?"

Hailey nodded to her mom, then approached Bea.
"Thanks for everything," she said softly.

"It was my pleasure to work with you, Hailey," Bea said.
"I hope maybe you and your mom will visit the set and
maybe you can do some art with me for the movie?"

Hailey's eyes lit up.

"Thanks again," Marjorie said, giving Beatrix a wink.

The mother and daughter headed off into the corridor.

Beatrix looked after them.

"Wow," Buck said.

"Yeah... wow," Beatrix echoed.

"I guess we'll have some planning to do on this road
trip," Buck said.

"I guess we will," Beatrix replied, still in a daze.

Buck wrapped his arms around her and pulled her in for
a long, lingering kiss.

When she was warm and trembly down to her toes, and
the waves of longing began to pull at her insides, Buck
pulled slightly away.

"We need to get home *now*," he whispered to her.

It was funny to think of home as a rented condo or a car

or a hotel. But wherever Buck was would be home for Beatrix - now and forever.

She flung her backpack over her shoulder and he wrapped his hand around hers. Together they walked through the convention center and out into the warm afternoon.

As they watched sunlight sparkle on the rippling surface of the Inner Harbor, Buck wrapped an arm around her shoulder, pulling her close and brushing the top of her head with a kiss.

"I love you so much, Beatrix," he whispered to her.

"I love you, Buck," she told him, smiling so hard it hurt her cheeks.

***

Thanks for reading Buck!
Keep reading for a sample of the next Stargazer Alien Mail Order Brides book: Solo.

Or grab your next book right now:
http://www.tashablack.com/stargazer.html

SOLO (SAMPLE)

1

CECILY

Cecily breathed in the delicious air of the meadow. She knew she was dreaming, but the details seemed more real than any dream she'd ever had. Crystal drops of dew sparkled on the leaves of the ancient maples and oaks surrounding the clearing, and a low mist clung to the ground as it always had at dawn.

Cecily hadn't been in the glade since she was a child. She and her friends had played here often, pretending to be the knights of the round table.

It was certainly the children's kingdom. The only other regular visitors were the Quakers in town, who used to come for their outdoor weddings. Cecily and her friends would sneak up and watch though the trees as the women in white cotton braided their long hair with ribbons and flowers, and the shirtless men danced and played their guitars under the afternoon sun. The most interesting part had always been the kiss at the end of the ceremony.

Though her mother called the Quakers hippies, Cecily herself couldn't imagine anything more romantic. It was half Shakespeare, half King Arthur.

Cecily had always imagined she would have her first kiss in the meadow.

It hadn't worked out that way, of course. Her actual first kiss had been at the town pool on a blisteringly hot day, with the scent of chlorine thick in the air. It hadn't been particularly romantic.

She'd always wanted a second chance at a first kiss in the glade.

But that could never happen. Aside from the obvious fact that her fist kiss was more than a few kisses ago, her Aunt Stacy told her the woods behind the high school had been leveled to make a parking lot for the new shopping center.

Of course, anything was possible in a dream.

She took a few steps forward. A rabbit hopped into the trees, but otherwise it was perfectly still, nothing but bird-song and the rustle of the breeze through the grass.

Cecily found that odd. There should be sounds coming from the shopping center, it couldn't be more than a couple of hundred yards away.

She closed her eyes and listened, but there was no hint of car engines or any other human interference.

The breeze caressed her hair like a lover and she opened her eyes again.

She wasn't alone anymore.

A man stood at the center of the glade. He was built like a god, tall, with broad shoulders, dark hair and piercing blue eyes.

There was something familiar about him, but she knew there had never been anyone like this in her hometown.

His hungry gaze beckoned and she went to him without hesitation.

The dewy grass tickled her bare toes as she closed the

distance between them. The air seemed to hum with electricity.

He lifted his hands, palms outward as she reached him and she placed her hands against his, knowing instinctively what he wanted from her.

The air around them swirled and out of the corner of her eye Cecily saw ghost images, like a sped-up special effect, herself and her friends as children, the weddings, the rabbits and the squirrels, the dawning and setting of a hundred translucent suns.

At first she was frightened, but the man sent waves of remembered comfort through the place where their hands touched.

And then it was something more than comfort.

The rush of memories receded as she looked up into his ocean blue eyes and lost herself to the agony of longing she saw there.

He leaned down slowly, as if afraid she would startle like one of the rabbits from her memory.

But Cecily had never craved anything more than this man's kiss.

When he pressed his mouth to hers, she saw a universe of stars spread out before her and heard the sound of distant chimes.

Flames of desire licked her insides and she kissed him back greedily, tasting the starlight of distant planets, feeling crystalline sand between her toes.

She was there and she was not there.

She was lost and found, tangled in the arms of this strange prince, in the enchanted glade of her childhood, panting with lust and yet transported beyond the confines of her body.

"Please," she whispered, not sure what she was begging for.

His mouth smiled against lips and she felt the press of his big body more firmly against hers. For all his gentleness the evidence of his own need pulsed hard and huge between them.

He pulled away slightly to look at her again.

She had the feeling again that she knew him, his identity was just out of the reach of her lust-addled mind.

"Cecily," he said softly.

She searched his face for clues.

"Cecily," he repeated, louder this time.

The glade began to fade away.

There was a knocking sound.

"Cecily," Kate's voice said.

Cecily turned and found she was in her bed, tangled in the sheets, gray dawn filtering through the blinds.

"I'm up, I'm up," she called to her roommate.

"Awesome," Kate called back. "We've got to get on the road soon. The guys are grabbing coffee."

The guys.

She knew who the mysterious stranger was now, of course.

She couldn't escape him, even in her dreams - Solo, the tall, dark and handsome, the gentleman, the alien. He was her ceaseless companion by day and her reckless lover by night.

Well, in her dreams at least.

Though she had every intention of resisting the attraction in real life, in these moments between sleep and waking she wondered how long she could realistically hold out.

Cecily stretched and unwound the sheets from around herself.

There was no point worrying about it today. Today was the day they all piled into the rented RV and began their journey west. She wouldn't be thrown into any dangerous scenarios for the duration of the cross country road trip. She and her two roommates, and the three aliens they had taken in, would be thrown together twenty-four-seven. They wouldn't have the time, or the opportunity, for any fooling around.

It was still unbelievable to Cecily to learn that there was life on other planets, let alone that she and her roommates had taken in three fugitive aliens. When the other two women began falling in love with the massive, hunky men, Cecily had decided to steel her heart against the temptation.

She lived a wonderful, carefree life, traveling the country to do make-up and special effects. She had a community of close colleagues, no shortage of friends with benefits when she wanted them, and zero intention of pinning her hopes and emotions on a man. Her mother had allowed herself to be hogtied by love and Cecily saw where that had wound her up.

So Solo was hot, so what? Cecily could have nearly any guy she wanted. Solo's impeccable manners and kind-hearted smile could make someone else happy. Cecily was her own woman.

Though the thought of Solo and another woman did give her a pang, Cecily would get over it. She always did. She had a handful of ex-friends-with-benefits who had settled down. There had been no hurt feelings or jealousy on her part, hell, she was "Aunt Cecily" to one or two of their kids. Solo would be no different.

Solo needed more than a fling. He needed to find a

woman to *click* with so he could become permanently human and thereby ease relations between Earth and his home planet, Aerie.

Maybe she could help him pick someone nice, someone who would appreciate him.

The thought troubled her somehow, and she pushed it aside, grabbing her robe and heading to the shower.

Her wild emotions would be tamed by a hot shower and a hotter cup of coffee.

It was going to be a fun day - she was sure of it. Cecily had always loved road trips.

***

Thanks for reading this sample of Solo!
Grab the rest of the story now:
http://www.tashablack.com/stargazer.html

TASHA BLACK STARTER LIBRARY

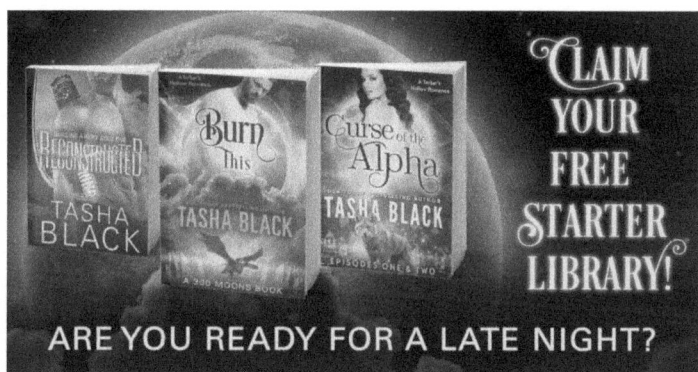

Packed with steamy shifters, mischievous magic, billionaire superheroes, and plenty of HEAT, the Tasha Black Starter Library is the perfect way to dive into Tasha's unique brand of Romance with Bite!

Get your FREE books now at tashablack.com!

ABOUT THE AUTHOR

Tasha Black lives in a big old Victorian in a tiny college town. She loves reading anything she can get her hands on, writing paranormal romance, and sipping pumpkin spice lattes.

Get all the latest info, and claim your FREE Tasha Black Starter Library at www.TashaBlack.com

Plus you'll get the chance for sneak peeks of upcoming titles and other cool stuff!

Keep in touch...
www.tashablack.com
authortashablack@gmail.com